The
Fragile
Flag

The Fragile Flag

Jane Langton

1 8  1 7

———————————— HARPER & ROW, PUBLISHERS ————————————

Cambridge, Philadelphia, San Francisco, London, Mexico City, São Paulo, Sydney

————————————————— NEW YORK —————————————————

The Fragile Flag
Text copyright © 1984 by Jane Langton
Illustration copyright © 1984 by Erik Blegvad
All rights reserved. No part of this book may be used or reproduced
in any manner whatsoever without written permission except in the
case of brief quotations embodied in critical articles and reviews. Printed
in the United States of America. For information address Harper & Row Junior
Books, 10 East 53rd Street, New York, N.Y. 10022. Published simultaneously
in Canada by Fitzhenry & Whiteside Limited, Toronto.
Designed by Joyce Hopkins
1 2 3 4 5 6 7 8 9 10
First Edition

Library of Congress Cataloging in Publication Data
Langton, Jane.
   The fragile flag.

   Summary: A nine-year-old girl leads a march of children from Massachusetts to Washington, in protest against
the President's new missile which is capable of destroy-
ing the earth.
   [1. Atomic weapons and disarmament—Fiction.
2. Disarmament—Fiction.   3. Arms control—Fiction.
4. Peace—Fiction]   I. Blegvad, Erik, ill.   II. Title.
PZ7.L2717Fr   1984   [Fic]   83-49471
ISBN 0-06-023698-1
ISBN 0-06-023699-X (lib. bdg.)

For Gabriel

Contents

──☆──

PART TWO

It is not an era of repose. We have used up all our inherited freedom. If we would save our lives, we must fight for them.

Henry Thoreau

PART ONE

The flag of our nation stands for a strong defense in a dangerous world. . . .

James R. Toby
President of the United States
The White House
Washington, D.C.

The flag means American people being friends with all the other people. . . .

Georgie Hall
Grade 4
Alcott School
Concord, Massachusetts

The Grove of Trees

— ☆ —

Georgie's family was like a grove of trees. There were four of them, standing tall around her, guarding her from sun and wind and snow and every kind of trouble.

Why, then, did Georgie suddenly take it into her head to march out from under their kindly shade and walk nearly half a thousand miles in the glaring heat of summer? Four hundred and fifty miles, carrying that big American flag!

It wasn't until the third week of May that Georgie Dorian Hall knew about the flag. Until then it was packed away in the attic, its stars and stripes folded softly against each other in the dark—star against star, stripe against stripe—deep in the bottom of a cardboard box.

Edward Hall didn't know about the flag either. Eddy was Georgie's stepcousin. Well, he was really more like her older brother, because they lived in the same house. Eddy was fascinated that springtime by automobiles, by suspensions and carburetors and transmissions. He was reading a book, *There's Adventure in Your Crankcase.* He certainly had no ambition to walk all the way from Concord, Massachusetts, to Washington, D.C.

Eddy's sister Eleanor was the oldest of the three children at No. 40 Walden Street.

This year, as always, Eleanor was enthralled by spring. As the sun warmed the ground and the grass gushed up from the wintry lawn, Eleanor came home every day after school and took off her heavy shoes and ran barefoot around the yard. On Saturdays she put on her school clothes again and walked around the town of Concord, looking for a summer job. Maybe she could work in the hardware store, and then Mr. Orth, her French teacher, might come in to buy a hammer or a toaster. Or she might get a cashier's job in the Star Market, where Robert Toby worked every summer, unpacking carrots and polishing eggplants.

Eleanor was interested in Robert Toby. Robert was a member of her own freshman class in high school, but he was really Eddy's friend, not hers. He never spoke to Eleanor in school. Running awkwardly around the gym during a basketball game with Wayland or Bedford or Acton-Boxborough, he never noticed Eleanor sitting loyally in the bleachers.

Eleanor tried to tell herself that she would have liked Robert even if his grandfather were *not* the President of the United States. But she knew in her heart that being the President's grandson gave Robert a lot of extra glamor. She just couldn't help being impressed by Robert's national importance. It was odd that it didn't seem to make any difference to Robert himself. Actually it was impossible to know what Robert thought about anything. He was tall and good-looking but he had an abstracted expression, like someone with his ear to a seashell. He was a modest boy, more interested in insects and butterflies than people.

Georgie, too, had other things on her mind those early weeks in May. She didn't know about the flag in the attic, and she paid no attention to what was happening in the world outside. She was busy with her new friend, Frieda Caldwell. Georgie and Frieda sat side by side in Miss Brisket's fourth-grade homeroom in the Alcott School. After school they always went to Frieda's house or Georgie's to spend the rest of the day. Frieda was small, with clouds of frizzy blond hair escaping from her pigtails. She had big glasses and a small nose and a mouth that was always talking.

Georgie was the same size as Frieda, but her wispy hair was no-color, and her arms and legs were like toothpicks. Georgie was quiet and obedient. Frieda was talkative and bossy. They were fast friends.

"Nutty little kids," Eddy would say. "All they do is giggle. Listen to that."

It was true. When they were together, everything seemed funny. If Georgie's shoe was untied, Frieda would double up in hysterics. If Frieda made a horrible face, Georgie would collapse hilariously on the bed. It was as if they shared a secret, a secret kept in whispers, a secret that slipped out in broad smiles and titters and laughter. The secret was their delight in each other's company. They were each other's first best friends.

Aunt Alex was relieved and glad. Her daughter Georgie had always been a sober little girl, with a way of taking things too hard. When Georgie was only four years old she had been desperate to learn to read. And last year she had tried to fly down the stairs. She had fallen down them over and over again in her eagerness to float in the air like a bird, like a goose, like a swan. She had covered herself with bruises.

Therefore Aunt Alex was delighted by the laughter from Georgie's room. She was pleased when she had to call up the stairs, "Georgie, not so much noise!" It was as if ordinary silliness had been building up in Georgie all the time, waiting for Frieda, and now it was coming out all at once.

Aunt Alex and Uncle Freddy were preoccupied too, that month of May. First they had to finish teaching their spring classes at Concord College. The college was their own school, and the classes met in their own house—in the parlor, or the kitchen, or the front hall, or outdoors on the lawn, or even in the branches of a tree in the backyard.

Next there was the new compaign to keep them busy, the fight against the President's Peace Missile. The Peace Missile was the President's latest nuclear weapon. Aunt Alex and Uncle Freddy were against it. They didn't want him to launch it into outer space. They didn't want him to build it at all. The *Concord Journal* was full of their plans for a bus trip to Washington, D.C. They were going to march up and down outside the White House carrying signs:

SAVE THE EARTH!
STOP THE PEACE MISSILE!
LET COMMON SENSE PREVAIL!

A lot of people were going along on the journey, a whole busload of friends and neighbors from Concord, Massachusetts.

"Maybe we'll start something," Uncle Freddy said, his voice ringing with hope. "A peaceful revolution against nuclear weapons. Maybe we'll begin it right now, right here, with this very busload of sixty Concord citizens." Uncle Freddy was spreading poster board all over the floor of the front porch. "After all, the first American Revolution began in Concord, when the Minutemen fought at the North Bridge. Don't you think the newspapers will take notice of these new Minutemen, our own Concord Patriots for Peace? *The Boston Globe* will send a reporter, I'll bet. And *The New York Times*. And all those news programs on television."

Eddy and Eleanor sat on the porch railing, watching Aunt Alex's paintbrush sweep boldly over the clean white cardboard. "Listen," Eleanor said eagerly, "what about Robert Toby? Why don't you ask him to come along? He could get you into the White House. After all, he *is* the President's grandson." Eleanor jumped down and stepped neatly around the big paper squares. "Do you want me to call him up?"

"Oh, no, Eleanor," said Aunt Alex, looking up quickly. "We can't ask Robert to do that. I'm sure he shares his grandfather's point of view."

Eddy snickered. "Robert Toby? Robert Toby

doesn't have a point of view. All he cares about is butterflies."

"Anyway," said Uncle Freddy firmly, "it's a grown-up trip. We might be arrested. It might be dangerous." Uncle Freddy was thinking of Henry Thoreau's night in jail. Henry had lived in Concord a long time back. He had been arrested for not paying his tax because he was against the Mexican War. Maybe this peaceful little band, too, would go to jail for opposing something worse than the Mexican War. Far, far more terrible! The end of the world! Uncle Freddy's brow wrinkled with anxiety.

"You'll remember to feed the cats?" said Aunt Alex to Eleanor as she climbed on the bus, clutching her posters. "And turn off the stove? And you won't fight? And you'll look after Georgie?"

"Of course, of course, don't *worry*."

"We Failed!"

—☆—

While Uncle Freddy and Aunt Alex were away, the flag still lay in the bottom of the box in the attic, folded silently against itself, out of the light. In the rest of the house, below the attic, Eddy and Eleanor took care of everything, and bossed Georgie, and stamped around the kitchen and the front hall. The timbers of the house trembled with their shouting; the hollow spaces were hot with retort, noisy with the slam of furious doors.

It was an old house, ugly and spacious, wrapped in friendly porches. On the outside it had a flimsy look, like an elderly person wasting a little away. Inside it was dark and comfortable, gleaming with the white busts of Henry Thoreau and Ralph Waldo Emerson and Louisa May Alcott. In the downstairs hall a tall bronze woman stood on the newel-post, holding a book in one hand and an electric light in the other. The light bulb was always flickering and brightening as the frayed old wiring pulled apart and came together again. From attic to cellar, the place was home.

Aunt Alex and Uncle Freddy were coming back on Sunday morning. After Sunday breakfast Eleanor had time to try on all the earrings in her collection. She stood in front of the mirror in her bedroom, staring at herself, and came to a decision. She would have her ears pierced. She really would. She definitely would.

Eddy was yelling up the stairs, "Hey, up there. It's time to go."

Eleanor tore off one pair of earrings and clamped on another. Then she plunged down the stairs and strode past Eddy, pushing Georgie in front of her out the door. Her earrings wobbled, and one fell off.

"Look at her," sneered Eddy, closing the door behind him. "One earring, just like Oliver Winslow."

"Oh, shut up," said Eleanor, snatching up her earring. Herding Georgie and Eddy through the gate, she began running ahead of them down the sidewalk to the corner of Everett Street. "Hurry up. If we're not there in time, they'll think we don't care."

Eddy loped after her. "It's no use anyway, the whole bus trip. All those people carrying signs around the White House, what difference will it make? The President's already got the money for the Peace Missile. He can do anything he wants."

"What do you mean, he's got the money?" Eleanor grabbed Georgie's hand and yanked her across the street. "They have to vote for it, don't they? The senators and congressmen have to vote the money, right?"

"No, they don't. Not if the President gets the money someplace else. It was on TV. The Pentagon has this Emergency Fund. There's enough money in the fund to build the new weapon and launch it into space. The President doesn't have to go through Congress at all."

"He *doesn't*?" Eleanor looked at Eddy, horrified, then turned swiftly and began rushing away from him.

Eddy stopped and stared at Eleanor's back as she galloped up Everett Street. "Hey, what are you going that way for?"

"It's shorter," snapped Eleanor.

"It is not shorter. It's just the same. Oh, I get it." Eddy snickered again, and began sprinting after his sister. "It's Robert Toby, right? Robert lives on Everett Street. Well, I'm sorry to inform you that Robert just happens to be in Washington right now with his grandfather, the President of the United States. Too bad."

Eleanor was disappointed, but she was careful not to look at Robert's house as she dragged Georgie past it. Out of the corner of her eye she could see Robert's mother sweeping the front porch. "Come on, Georgie, run!" Then Eleanor glanced back at Eddy. "Listen, you mean the senators and congressmen don't get to vote on the Peace Missile at all?"

"That's right. That's what Derek Cherniak, the TV anchorman in Washington, said on the news. So pretty soon the new bomb will be up there, pointed at the earth, all souped up with nuclear chain reactions, ready to go *KABOOM* when anybody pushes the button, or whenever the wires get crossed or something."

Georgie was racing along beside Eleanor on her matchstick legs, looking back and forth from Eleanor to Eddy. "What happens then?" she said timidly.

Eleanor glared at Georgie and gripped her arm too hard. "Well, there are all these scientists— you know, big experts—and half of them say it will ignite the atmosphere, and the other half say it won't."

"Ignite—?"

"Set fire to it."

Eddy made it clear. "And then, *spppffffttt,* that's it, the end of the human race." He clutched at his throat. *"The eeeeeeennnnnnnnd of the woooooorrrrrrlllllld!"* He staggered crazily along the sidewalk, pretending to cough and choke, then straightened up. "Of course, the other half say it would just blow up the Soviet Union and any other countries that might just happen to be in the way at the time."

Georgie pulled away from Eleanor and stopped short and gasped, "But President Toby can't do that. He mustn't."

Eddy patted her on the head. "Well, you tell him that, Georgie. You just tell him that."

"Listen, Georgie, where have you been?" said Eleanor. "Haven't you been paying any attention at all? That's what Uncle Fred and Aunt Alex went to Washington *for.* Didn't you see their signs? That's what they were doing yesterday. They were marching around the White House, carrying all those signs."

"Oh," said Georgie, her face pale, "I didn't know." She began to run again, trying to keep up with Eleanor, scurrying stiffly on her spidery legs.

They were only just in time. As they came panting to the corner of Thoreau Street and Sudbury Road, the chartered bus was already there, lumbering slowly to a stop, its brakes wheezing.

They stood back and watched the passengers descend.

The Concord Patriots for Peace looked tired. They had spent two nights on the bus and a long day in ,the city of Washington, marching up and down. Their faces were gray and drawn. Their signs, which had looked so gay and defiant when they boarded the bus two days ago, were crumpled and streaked with dirt. The Concord Patriots nodded to Eddy and Eleanor and Georgie, and then, wordlessly, without saying good-bye to each other, they trailed across the street and climbed into their cars and drove away.

Aunt Alex and Uncle Freddy were the last ones off the bus.

"Oh, children," said Aunt Alex. She thumped her bag on the sidewalk and brushed back her tangled hair. Uncle Freddy smiled grimly. His coat was wrinkled. His hair, too, was wild, sticking out from his head.

The doors of the bus closed silently, and it moved away, its big windows empty and dark.

"Well, what happened?" said Eddy, picking up the bag.

Aunt Alex took Georgie's hand and started

walking up Sudbury Road. "Well, the truth is," she said flatly, "we failed."

Uncle Freddy explained. "We were turned away at the White House gate," he said. "There was a guard there. I told him we had a petition with hundreds of signatures. We had been promised a hearing. 'Well, you're having it,' he said. 'You're not on my list.' And he took the petition and put it in a box with a lot of other stuff, including a big toy rabbit. I guess it was left over from Easter. Maybe somebody wanted to give the President a big Easter rabbit." Uncle Freddy inspected his finger as he limped along the sidewalk after Aunt Alex. "Alex, dear, remember what Thoreau said about wooden men, with wooden heads and hearts? I swear, when I gave the guard our petition, when I put it into his hand, I got a sliver. Did you notice, dear, how much his eyes were like knotholes?"

Aunt Alex smiled forlornly. But Eleanor was disappointed. "You mean you didn't even get arrested?"

"Oh, no," said Uncle Freddy. "The police didn't even give us a second glance. They were perfect gentlemen. They held up traffic so we could cross the street."

"No kidding." Eddy was chagrined. He had been picturing rebellious heroism on the part of

Uncle Freddy and Aunt Alex, an assault over the White House fence, with policemen hurling tear gas at them and unleashing their attack dogs. "We watched the news last night," Eddy said. "But nobody mentioned you people at all."

"Because we just completely failed," said Aunt Alex again, heavily. "And that's the truth of it."

"But what about your signs?" said Georgie earnestly. "Didn't the President look out the window and read your signs?"

Uncle Freddy shook his head. "I suspect the President was taking a nap."

"Well, anyway, you're home just in time to hear his speech," said Eleanor. "He's giving a big speech this afternoon on TV."

"So we heard," said Aunt Alex dryly. Then she drew Georgie away from the curb as a car pulled up beside them and rolled noisily to a stop.

It was an ugly car, an enormous old heap, a beat-up sedan, its metal body rusting out. The green surface had faded and filmed over with a dull rainbow bloom. The muffler hung down. The exhaust pipe rattled on the road. The right rear fender was crushed.

"Oh, no," murmured Eleanor, closing her eyes, "not Oliver Winslow."

A familiar face was looking out from the driv-

er's seat, grinning at them, a single piratical earring dangling from one ear.

"Hey, Oliver, wow, where'd you get this piece
of junk?" Eddy leaned in through the rear window, inspecting the burst seat covers. "What is
it?"

"Chevy Impala," explained Oliver. He revved
the engine. Something squealed. "Listen to that.
You hear that? Fan belt's slipping."

"Oh, is that it?" said Eddy. "What's that clattering noise?"

The engine roared, and they could all hear the
ominous rattle. Smoke seeped from under the
hood. "Jeez," said Oliver. "I better give her some
oil. The valves are probably fried." He smiled
proudly, the owner of fried valves and squealing
fan belt and everything else—a gasoline engine,
a chassis, a dashboard, four wheels and a spare,
the works. "You people want a ride?"

"Why, sure," said Eddy, trying to yank open
the bent back door.

"You gotta get in on the other side."

"Not me," said Eleanor. "I'm not getting in that
thing. I'll bet it smells."

But Aunt Alex and Georgie were climbing into
the front to sit beside Oliver, and Uncle Freddy
was telling Eddy to move over. Reluctantly Eleanor

squeezed onto the backseat beside Uncle Freddy.

The car was grubby but roomy, and it carried them safely to No. 40 Walden Street, the engine grinding all the way.

At home they climbed out and thanked Oliver. Then Georgie and Eleanor and Uncle Freddy and Aunt Alex went up the walk to the house, leaving Eddy and Oliver bowed under the open hood.

On the front porch Aunt Alex paused and looked down at the wooden floorboards. She could still see the jolly stroke of her paintbrush where it had swept right off the paper as she finished the last letter of the message on her poster,

LET COMMON SENSE PREVAIL!

She pulled open the door and stalked into the house. "We failed," she said again. "The fact is, we failed."

The Two Flags

— ☆ —

With solemn faces and folded arms they sat in front of the television set in the kitchen and watched the President's speech.

It wasn't about the Peace Missile. It was about a new presidential American flag and a contest for the children of the nation.

Derek Cherniak, the famous television newsman, introduced President Toby. "And now," he said dramatically, "the President of the United States."

There he was, the President, with his familiar balding forehead and sandy hair and grizzled mustache.

Then Eleanor sucked in her breath, and Eddy whistled gleefully. Behind the President stood Robert Toby, holding the American flag. Behind Robert, tulips and irises were blooming in the White House Rose Garden.

The President was explaining his new flag. Taking one corner, he backed away from his grandson, so that all of it could be seen at once. It was a very fancy American flag made of satin. The stars were glittering with gold sequins, and the words *God Bless America* had been written boldly across the stripes in gold sparkles. The flag was bordered with a gold fringe, and on the top of the staff crouched a gold eagle with its beak open wide as if it were tearing something apart.

Then the President dropped his corner of the flag and stepped forward to fill the screen.

The new flag, he said, was to be carried by children.

"Some of you young people out there, watching me right now, will have the honor of bearing this flag. I hope every young person in the country in the fourth, fifth, sixth, seventh, and eighth grades will write me a letter explaining what the flag of our country means to you. I know what it means to *me*," said the President, pointing at himself. "To me the flag stands for strength."

"Oh, dear," murmured Aunt Alex, clenching her hands in her lap.

"But I want to know what it means to *you*." Smiling, the President pointed his finger at the camera. "Here in Washington we will read all the letters, every single one, and then we will choose one young person from each of the fifty states to come to the White House in turn, to do what my grandson is doing now, to be the official bearer of the presidential flag, to join me on errands of state, to hold the colors high!"

Eddy laughed. The President was turning his head to look proudly at Robert, but at that moment Robert had let the flag sag a little, and he was gazing straight up over his head.

"There's a butterfly up there, I'll bet," said Eddy.

"Robert?" said the President.

Robert's head dropped, and he jerked the flag upright. The President went on with his talk. "Only fifty young people will be chosen. . . ."

Eleanor stared at Robert as the President went on and on. She tried to imagine the millions and millions of people who were looking at him too, all over the country, right now. It was hard to realize how famous he was. Somehow Robert's famousness made him terribly attractive. It made you want to know him, to be his friend, to have him like you, to like you best of all.

The speech was over. Derek Cherniak was back again, looking ruggedly handsome, explaining that it was time for a commercial message. Then the pretty face of a little girl filled the screen. She was drinking orange soda through a straw.

"Look," said Georgie, "Veronica Glassmore."

Eddy and Eleanor made disgusted faces. "Yuck," said Eddy.

"Ugh," said Eleanor.

Veronica Glassmore was as famous as Derek Cherniak, as famous as Robert Toby, as famous as the President. She had long black hair and huge green eyes. Now she picked up another bottle of orange soda and offered it to Eleanor, to Eddy, to Georgie, to everybody in the country. The bottle filled the screen.

"Gee, thanks," said Eddy cynically, and switched the set off.

Uncle Freddy gazed moodily at the empty gray screen that had shown them the President and Robert and Veronica Glassmore. "He's stolen it," he said. "He's kidnapped it."

"Kidnapped what?" said Eleanor.

"The flag, the American flag." Uncle Freddy was indignant. "It's not his flag."

"Of course not," said Aunt Alex.

"It's everybody's flag. It's yours, Eddy. It's yours, Eleanor."

"Right, right," said Eddy and Eleanor.

"It's Georgie's."

"Mine?" said Georgie in surprise.

"It's yours, it's mine, it's everybody's." Uncle

Freddy jumped up. "Look, I'll show you. We have a flag. Our own American flag. Wait right here. Don't go away. I'll be right back."

Uncle Freddy galloped up two flights of stairs and stood panting in the attic doorway, looking for the right box. Yes, there it was, way back in the shadows under the eaves.

He dragged it out and clawed at the string. Then he opened the flaps and looked inside.

The box was full of precious things. On top, wrapped in tissue paper, was the wedding dress that had been worn by his sister Lily. It was made of lace like a tissue of snowflakes. Beneath the dress lay the stereoscope that had taken the children on all those queer journeys a couple of years ago. Under the stereoscope was a length of charred rope that had once been part of the swing in the old summerhouse. And what was this small hard object, wadded up in newspaper like a priceless treasure? It was the cheap little rubber ball that had meant so much to Georgie.

Carefully Uncle Freddy lifted everything out of the box until there was nothing left but a big piece of folded cloth in the very bottom. Tenderly he removed it and draped it over his shoulder and put everything else back. Then he went downstairs again, carrying the flag.

There was an astonished silence in the kitchen as he unfolded it and shook it out, holding it high so that the field of stars was at the top and the stripes hung straight down. The flag covered Uncle Freddy from shoulder to toe.

It was old, so old that the woolen threads were nearly transparent. The red stripes were faded, the white stripes were the color of old bone. But the fat stars were surely as white as they had ever been, scattered on the dark blue of the square in the upper left-hand corner.

Georgie stared at the flag in awe. Eddy picked up one edge and displayed a hole. "Look at that. A bullet hole, what do you want to bet? And blood! You see that spot? That's blood."

Eleanor refused to believe it. "That's not a bullet hole, stupid, it's a moth hole. And that's not blood. It's just, you know, a spot. Old cloth, it gets these spots." She snatched the corner of the flag from Eddy, then looked at Aunt Alex in apology. "I'm sorry. It tore."

Aunt Alex shook her head in reproof. "Goodness, Eleanor, you must be more careful."

Uncle Freddy draped the flag over the curtain rod at the window. "I wonder how old it really is," he said.

Georgie spoke up knowingly. "You can tell by

counting the stars," she said. "You know, one for each state as it joined the union." She started to count, then lost her place and started over. *One, two, three, four, five, six, seven*—Oh, it was too hard! How could she possibly count all the stars? There were too many. It was like counting the stars in the sky. Then a puff of air from the window pushed against the flag, and it blew forward and enveloped Georgie. For a moment she floated free, suspended in the Milky Way, surrounded by clouds that were really millions and millions of tiny points of light.

It was only for a moment, and then the flag fell back, and Georgie's feet were once more firmly planted on the linoleum floor of the kitchen. She caught her breath and grasped the back of a chair.

Eleanor too had been trying to count the stars. But now she put her hand to her forehead. "I-I can't," she said. "They won't hold still." For Eleanor the stars were like an enormous flock of birds, rising from the ground in flurries, settling and taking off again, over and over. And how could you possibly count that?

Eddy was lost too. "It's crazy," he said, staring at the flag. "For a minute I felt funny. Really queer." For Eddy the stars were like schools of fish, darting this way and that in sunlit water.

They stood back in frustration, staring at the flag.

"Never mind," said Uncle Freddy. "Where shall we put it? Outdoors? We could hang it from the roof of the porch."

"Oh, no, it's too old and delicate for that," said Aunt Alex. She took the flag down from the window and held it against the wall behind the ironing board. "No," she said, gathering it up again. "Not dignified enough."

They wandered out into the hall, looking for a place to hang the flag.

"We could use it for a curtain in the parlor door," said Eleanor, "instead of those old pieces of velvet."

Aunt Alex shook her head. "Not respectful enough," she said.

Then Georgie had an idea. "Why don't we hang it from there?" she said, pointing to the bronze lady on the staircase.

They all said, "Of course."

It was easy. The flag had metal grommets at one end. Uncle Freddy tied the uppermost grommet to the bronze hand that held the light bulb, and the lowest to the hand that held the book. The flag draped over the woman's tall form like a gown, and trailed almost to the floor. She looked like the Statue of Liberty. Then someone burst in the door, and the gust of wind lifted the flag until it billowed wide.

"Wow," said Oliver Winslow, taken by surprise. "That's beautiful."

They all stood speechless and looked at it. The red and white stripes seemed brighter. In the wind from the open door the flag fluttered and tossed and dipped and curled. The stars tumbled on the field of blue. At the top, the light bulb in the bronze woman's upflung hand seemed to shine more brilliantly than usual, as if a higher wattage were running through the wire. The ragged ends of the flag quivered playfully.

Georgie stared at it and made a vow. She would write a letter to the President and tell him what the flag meant to her. It would be the best letter she could write. The President would read it, and then maybe he would understand. And then maybe he would stop building that terrible Peace Missile. And then the whole world would be safe, all the people and the animals, and the oceans and the forests.

Georgie's vow was like a promise in blood, an oath triple-locked and sealed. When Georgie crossed her heart it was crossed forever, like the vows sworn by knights on the bones of saints in days of old.

No one knew what she was thinking. If she could have played her vow on the piano, her passionate purpose could have been heard. If she could have painted it in a picture, it might have been seen. But it was only in her mind, and therefore it was invisible.

"Where are you going, Georgie?" said her mother.

"Just upstairs," said Georgie. She went up to her room and closed the door.

The Most Important Thing

— ☆ —

At nine o'clock sharp on Monday morning Miss Brisket told the fourth grade about the President's letter-writing contest. She wrote the subject of the contest on the board:

WHAT THE FLAG OF MY COUNTRY
MEANS TO ME

"Now," said Miss Brisket, gathering her courage, prepared for disappointment, "how many of you boys and girls would like to write to the President of the United States?"

And then she was astonished. She wondered if the children had heard her properly.

All their hands were up. They were looking at her soberly.

Georgie was astonished too. She looked at

Frieda. Frieda's glasses were flashing fiercely in the sunlight. "You too?" whispered Georgie.

"Me too," said Frieda.

Miss Brisket was beaming. She was really pleased. "Well, then, good! Now, class, let me explain the schedule. Your letters are to be turned in on Thursday, so that I can mail all of them together on Friday in a big envelope. They must be postmarked no later than Friday. That's the rule."

But on Tuesday, Wednesday, and Thursday, Georgie was not in school. She was sick in bed, really sick, too sick to write a letter to the President.

On Friday morning she felt better. Her mother let her get up and put on her clothes and sit at her desk. Georgie took a page out of her notebook and wrote,

> *Dear Mr. President,*
> *To me the flag of my country means . . .*

But then she was stuck. She stared out the window at the birds in the yard. They were flying back and forth between two trees in short flights. When they landed in one tree they changed their minds and flew back to the other tree. There was a continual silent coming and going.

Georgie watched the birds and despaired. What was it she had been so eager to say to the President? What did the flag mean to her, really? What was the most important thing about the country—that was what the letter was supposed to be about—the most important thing of all?

She dug her pencil into the paper, hoping for the first word. The point of the pencil snapped.

The pencil sharpener was in the kitchen. Sighing, Georgie got up and went downstairs saying to herself, *The most important thing, the most important thing.*

It was a mild day. The front door was open. As Georgie turned at the bottom of the stairs, her mother opened the back door to carry the laundry into the yard. Immediately there was a tug of air between the front door and the back. The old flag hanging from the arms of the bronze woman on the newel-post lifted gently in the breeze and reached out to curl around Georgie. Once again she found herself enclosed in a swaying tent of red and blue and white. She stopped and waited, entranced. It was like standing in a rainbow. Through the woven threads she could see the open door and the front porch and the green grass and the lush growth along the Mill Brook across the street.

But then to her surprise she heard the beat of a drum, and saw something strange across the field beyond the brook. Men were hurrying along Lexington Road. They looked like old-fashioned citizens of Concord, people who had lived in the town long ago. They were carrying long guns, muskets, over their shoulders. And then Georgie understood. They were Concord Minutemen. They were getting ready to defend the town against the British. She had learned all about it in school.

And then the Minutemen disappeared down the road and the drumming stopped and Georgie blinked. It was only a flick of a second before she opened her eyes again, but while they had been shut, a whole lifetime had gone by, years and years. Someone was climbing up the bank of the Mill Brook, carrying his hat upside down in one hand and a pickerelweed flower in the other.

Georgie recognized him right away. It was Henry Thoreau, Uncle Freddy's beloved Henry Thoreau. There was a plaster bust of Henry right beside Georgie in the hall. He was an old friend. As Georgie watched, delighted, a frog jumped out of Henry's hat and hopped away in the grass. Henry laughed and let it go.

And then Georgie gasped. The bright vision of the Mill Brook was disappearing in a sudden flash of light. A rush of hot wind burst in the door and threw her to her knees. And then there was a roaring explosion that thundered and thundered as though it would never end. Looking up, Georgie caught a glimpse of a new world, and trembled in fear.

There was nothing left of Concord but ashes and the charred stumps of trees. The sky was seething with dark clouds. The old houses across the field were gone, vanished utterly. The water of the brook was dried up. Gray flakes fell from the sky, then lifted and swirled and fell again to cover the ground. And then, as Georgie watched in silent horror, the shivering flag through which she had seen such wonderful and terrible things released her. It flapped once and fell back against the railing of the stairs.

Georgie lifted her hands gratefully. Once again the sun was shining blandly on the green grass and the scrawny barberry hedge and the marshy jungle beside the brook. Across the field the old houses rose blocky and solid along Lexington Road. The town was restored. Concord was back to normal.

But the flag was on fire! Flames were consuming one end, eating into the vivid stripes, running up one edge to the field of stars. Snatching up the rug that lay in front of the door, Georgie wrapped it around the flag and muffled the flames. Then she stood back with the rug in her hands, breathing hard. The fire was out. The flag hung slack. Its edges were singed and blackened, its bright colors faded as though it were pale with dread.

Shaking, Georgie put the rug back in front of the door, and then she went to the kitchen and sharpened her pencil, turning the crank with trembling fingers. Her mother came in the back door, swinging the empty laundry basket.

Georgie looked at her dolefully. Dropping the basket, her mother reached out to brush away the gray film that clung to Georgie's cheeks like ashes. "Georgie, dear, are you all right?"

Georgie opened her mouth to tell her mother about the terrible flash of light, and the thundering explosion, and the grim landscape under the boiling sky. But it had been too overwhelming. Shaking her head, she turned away and walked upstairs with her sharpened pencil, thinking about what she had seen.

It was important then, this place where she lived. Its history was important, and so were the great men who had lived here and written books. Even the frogs and wild flowers of Concord, Massachusetts, were important. So that awful thing mustn't happen, that ghastly thing she had seen at the end, that terrible flash of light. It must never happen on the earth, that sky as black as night and those gray flakes falling from the sky!

Georgie's mother stood at the foot of the stairs and listened to the sound of Georgie's door quietly closing. Poor child! What was it now that was disturbing her so bitterly?

Too Late!

— ☆ —

By the time Georgie finished her letter to the President, the sun was no longer shining on the windowsill, lighting up her room. It had moved around to the back of the house.

"Georgie?" Her mother put her head in the door. "Would you like something to eat?"

"What time is it?" said Georgie, startled.

"Almost five o'clock. Frieda called. I told her you were busy."

Georgie was horrified. She jumped up from her chair. "But my letter!" she said. "It has to be mailed today. And the post office closes at five o'clock." She snatched up her letter and looked around wildly for an envelope. Her mother found one, but it was five minutes before Georgie catapulted out of the house and raced along Walden Street in the direction of the post office.

She was too late. The post office was closed.

Georgie stood on the steps, looking at the locked door, her letter tightly gripped in her hand. If she mailed it tomorrow, the people in Washington would look at the postmark and throw the envelope away unopened. She had missed the contest entirely. But there was another way to get the letter to the President of the United States.

Georgie turned away and went down the steps slowly, making up her mind, fashioning another link to the resolute chains of her vow. She could give the letter to the President with her own hand. She could carry it all the way from Concord, Massachusetts, to the White House in Washington, D.C., and deliver it in person.

Grimly Georgie stalked home.

She had to do it. She would do it. She would walk all the way. She would start tomorrow, early in the morning.

The Fiery Furnace

— ☆ —

The driveway to the basement entrance of the
Executive Office Building in Washington, D.C.,
was choked with mail trucks. The trucks were
loaded with mailbags. The mailbags were stuffed
with letters from fourth, fifth, sixth, seventh, and
eighth graders in every state in the union. The
bags were dumped out of the trucks and slung
into a chute and carried to the judging room.
There they were sorted and tossed into huge bins
labeled *Alaska, Maine, Louisiana, Kansas.* There
were bins for all the fifty states.

Mrs. Linda Goodspeed was in charge. Mrs.
Goodspeed had worked out an efficient system
for judging the letter-writing contest. Her first
decision had been the most sweeping. She had
made up her mind at once that it would be impossible to read more than a few hundred letters

from each state. Therefore only one mailbag from Massachusetts was dumped on the long table where she and her assistant judges were working.

"I suppose every one of the poor dears thinks the President himself is going to read their letters," she said as she shuffled through the pile. One of the sorters was suspending another Massachusetts mailbag over the table, ready to shake it out. "Oh, no, stop," cried Mrs. Goodspeed. "That's quite enough. I'm sure we'll find a simply marvelous Massachusetts letter in this batch from Springfield." Picking up an envelope, Mrs. Goodspeed whisked her letter opener along the top— *rrrriiiiip!*—plucked out the letter, ran her eyes swiftly down the page, made a face, and tossed it aside. "Another protest. Isn't it strange! Half the letters are against the Peace Missile. Half the children seem to think the flag of their country means a nation without a proper system of defense. I suspect," said Mrs. Goodspeed darkly, "their parents put them up to it. Well, that kind of letter isn't going to win. I decided that at once, in consultation with the President." Mrs. Goodspeed opened a second letter from Springfield and made another face.

"What shall I do with all these other bags from Massachusetts?" said the boy with the mailbag. "I mean, there's this whole big bin here, chock-full of them."

"Oh, they all go into the furnace. Didn't you see what happened to the Alaska letters?" Mrs. Goodspeed flapped her hands. "Out, out, out! How could we possibly read them all? It would take a year."

And therefore all the letters from the town of Concord went unread, all the letters from the Alcott School, the Thoreau School, and Willard, and Peabody, and Sanborn, including Frieda's letter and Eddy's. They were tossed into the fiery furnace in the basement of the Executive Office Building, and burned to a crisp.

She Would Claw Her Way Out through Stone

— ☆ —

Georgie's mother stared at her daughter.

There she stood, small and pale, her face remote, her eyes fixed on something far away. Behind her loomed a huge knapsack. Below the knapsack and the puffy vest and the pair of denim shorts, Georgie's thin legs were like the stalks of pale underwater flowers. She was bristling with useful things. There was a flashlight in the pocket of her shorts, bananas in the pockets of her vest, and a road map sticking out of the neck of her shirt. Over her shoulder she carried the old flag from the attic.

"Where did you get the staff for the flag?" said Georgie's mother. Dazed and disconcerted, Aunt Alex was trying to think, wondering what to do in this unexpected crisis. "Oh, I know," she said, her lips white, "it's the handle of the old floor mop, isn't it?"

"Yes," said Georgie, glancing up at the top of the staff, where the metal clamping device for the mop took the place of a proper knob or a gilded spear point or a gold American eagle. "I decided it would be okay to borrow it, because you've got that new squeeze-mop now."

"Oh, yes, dear, of course. But, dear child, have you really thought it through?" Aunt Alex didn't know what to say. How could she persuade Georgie to give up her mad notion of walking all the way to Washington? She knew her daughter very well. She had seen that look of solemn purpose on her face before. Normally Georgie was the most tractable of the three children, the most obedient. But there had been several times in Georgie's life when she had made up her mind about something, when she had been transfixed by an idea that overwhelmed everything else, that hummed and buzzed in all her stringy nerves, that convulsed her whole body with tenacious determination. And then, whatever she needed to do, she did it. It wasn't because she was spoiled. It was because she was driven.

Aunt Alex sighed, and lifted a trembling hand to her mouth, numb with anxiety. Of course she could say no to Georgie, and forbid her to go, and lock her in her room. But what good would that do? If the walls of Georgie's room were solid rock, she would claw her way out through stone.

"So I'd better say good-bye now," said Georgie.

"Wait!" Georgie's mother flung out her hand. "I know what to do. I'll come too. I'll come with you."

But Georgie's face was stern. "No," she said. "That wouldn't work."

Her mother winced. Georgie was right. The grown-ups had failed, that was what she meant. It was Georgie's turn to try. If her mother came along, it would spoil it.

But Washington was so very far away! With clear foresight, Aunt Alex saw the hundreds of miles that separated Georgie from her destination, hundreds of miles of burning heat, of endless highway, of rain and cold. She saw the danger of the rushing cars, and the greater danger of those that slowed down and stopped beside the walking child. And at the same time she knew that Georgie would have the power to do it, to walk the whole way, to accomplish what she was setting out to do. But Aunt Alex was afraid.

"Oh, Georgie, how will you eat? Where will you sleep? What if something goes wrong? What if you get sick?"

Georgie patted the zippered breast pocket of her vest. "I'll call you every day. I've got the money

I saved. I've got my sleeping bag." She turned around to display the tight roll strapped under her knapsack.

"But, Georgie, haven't you got enough money for the bus? Why don't you take the bus?"

Georgie shook her head firmly. "I've got to walk," she said. "If I came on the bus, the President wouldn't see me. But if I walk all the way, maybe he'll let me in." She reached up to kiss her mother. "Well, so long, then. Say good-bye to Uncle Freddy for me. And Frieda, and Eddy and Eleanor."

Paralyzed, Georgie's mother stood in the doorway and watched Georgie go through the front gate and turn her shoulders smartly in the direction of Route 2. Georgie didn't look like a girl with a knapsack, carrying a flag. She looked like a knapsack and a flag miraculously bobbing along the street, supported on a couple of toothpicks.

Then Aunt Alex came to her senses. She ran after Georgie, crying, "Wait, wait."

Georgie turned obediently and waited for her mother.

"Listen, Georgie," said Aunt Alex, kneeling on the sidewalk, gripping Georgie's arms, "Eleanor and Eddy will go with you. Come back now and let Uncle Freddy work out a route. The safest

way. Did you know you can't walk on the turn-
pike? It's against the law."

Georgie thought it over. Then to her mother's
relief she smiled, and said, "Well, okay," and walked
back to the house with her mother. "Tomorrow,"
she said firmly. "No later than tomorrow. I've got
to get started. I've got to get there, you see, as
soon as I can."

Ruefully Aunt Alex explained it to Uncle Freddy
when he came home from his day at the Boston
Public Library. "She has to talk to the President,
you see. She thinks he'll suddenly realize how
wrong he's been all along."

Uncle Freddy understood the gravity of the
situation at once. He, too, knew the frail authority
of Georgie's will. His face turned ashen as he,
too, saw that there was nothing they could do to
stop her. "And perhaps," he said feebly, "she's
right. I mean, if anyone could persuade the man,
it would have to be someone like Georgie." Then
Uncle Freddy's face took on the rapt look that
meant he was going to quote from his hero, Henry
Thoreau. "Remember what Henry said about the
power of one honest man? What about the power
of one honest girl? 'It matters not how small the

beginning.' " Then Uncle Freddy glanced through the parlor curtain at the pair of spindly legs descending the staircase. "I mean, look at her! There's a small beginning, if ever there was one."

Eleanor was flabbergasted when Uncle Freddy and Aunt Alex broke the news. She couldn't believe it. Eleanor had been shopping. She had bought a new blow-dryer for her hair. Now she dumped the package on the kitchen table. "She's going to do *what?*" She stared at Georgie, her mouth agape. "She's going to walk a thousand miles? And you want *me* to go along?"

"Not a thousand," said Georgie, her face somber, her jaw set. "Four hundred and fifty, that's all."

Eleanor rolled her eyes at the ceiling. "Oh, *only* four hundred and fifty. Oh, *well*, then. *Any* nine-year-old child can walk four hundred and fifty *miles.*"

"You'll have to pace yourself, Georgie," said Uncle Freddy, looking at her anxiously. "Have you figured out how long it will take? Do you know how many miles you can walk in a day?"

Georgie had figured it out. "Six weeks," she said quickly. "I can walk nine or ten miles a day. Well, I can really do a lot more than that, but I thought I'd start slow and work up to it." Georgie sat stiffly at the table, gripping the mop handle of the flag.

"I can't believe this," said Eleanor. "I just can't believe it. You're not going to let her go?"

Uncle Freddy looked at his knees without speaking. Aunt Alex turned away to spoon out a dish of cat food. She put it on the floor, and called, "Here, kitty, kitty."

The front door banged. It was Eddy, home from a high school baseball game. He was exuberant. "We won," he said loudly, bursting into the kitchen. "You should have seen Robert Toby. He brought in the winning run."

"He did?" Eleanor's face reddened with hero worship. "Honestly?"

"Oh, he didn't deserve it. It was an accident. He was looking the other way. The ball bounced off his bat."

"Oh," said Eleanor. She glowered at Eddy. "Listen, wait till you hear the crazy thing that's happening around here."

But Eddy didn't think it was crazy. When he heard about Georgie's plan, he agreed at once. He had no qualms. "I'll come," he said. Eddy was sick of school.

"But, Georgie, what good will it do?" pleaded

Eleanor, still thunderstruck. "You don't think one crazy little kid is going to change the mind of the President of the United States?" Then Eleanor reached across the table and patted Georgie's hand apologetically. "Just kidding, Georgie," she said, and reminded herself to be more careful what she said. The trouble with Georgie was that she took things hard. They didn't just roll off the outside of her in a few tantrums and a fit of crying. They went all the way to the middle. And for a skinny little kid, Georgie had an awful lot of middle. She was about ten miles deep. Eleanor picked up the trailing end of the flag. "The American flag isn't supposed to touch the floor," she said in mock seriousness. "Did you know that, Georgie? It isn't patriotic."

The cloth was warm in Eleanor's fingers, and thin as a handkerchief. She fingered the scorched edge. Had it been like that before, all blackened along the hem?

Suddenly, Eleanor knew what to do. "I'll come too," she said impulsively.

Georgie clapped her hands and jumped up. Then they all got to work on the problem of what they should take along. Georgie unpacked her knapsack to show them what she was bringing.

"Water," said Eddy. "A thermos of water. I'll

bet you didn't think of that."

"Oh, no, I forgot," said Georgie.

Aunt Alex and Uncle Freddy were relieved. Eleanor was fourteen, a sensible girl on the whole. Edward was a strong, practical boy of twelve. In their company Georgie would be much safer than if she went alone.

A Company of Friends

— ☆ —

"Robert?" said Eleanor, holding the phone in a grip of steel.

"Who's this?"

"It's Eleanor."

"Oh."

"Listen, we're going on a march. I just wondered if you'd like to come along." Hastily Eleanor explained Georgie's plan. She knew she sounded befuddled.

Robert said, "Oh," again. And then, to Eleanor's astonishment, he said, "Well, okay."

"What did you say?" said Eleanor.

"I said, I guess I'll come."

Eleanor was stunned. She hung up. Then she had to call Robert back and explain when they were leaving and what he had to bring with him. "What about your mother? Will she let you go?"

"My mother? Oh." There was a pause. Robert seemed to be thinking it over. "It's all right," he said. "It'll be okay."

Eleanor wondered how Robert would persuade his mother, Mrs. Toby, to let him walk to Washington. His mother was the President's daughter-in-law. She was a widow. Like her son Robert, she didn't seem to be stuck-up just because she was so closely related to the President of the United States. Like Robert, too, she was a little vague and absentminded. Maybe she would think Robert was going on a long nature hike.

Anyway, it was staggering to think that she, Eleanor Hall, was going to be walking four hundred and fifty miles in the company of Robert Toby, the President's grandson. Eleanor ran upstairs and undid the buckles of her knapsack and stuffed her new blow-dryer in on top of everything else.

Eddy saw what she was doing. "What a jerk," he said. "There aren't any electrical outlets beside the road, you dummy. But, I don't know, maybe"— Eddy struck a comic pose—"maybe you can plug it into a tree. You know, maybe you'll find a lot of trees between here and Washington all fitted up with electrical outlets."

So Eleanor reluctantly left out the blow-dryer.

She packed a bag of big curlers instead.

Frieda Caldwell was coming too. At first her mother was horrified, but then Frieda talked her into it. Frieda was a strong talker. She had been the boss in her family since she was four days old.

Georgie was thrilled. Her lonely walk to Washington had become a marching company of friends. She didn't mind waiting an extra day, while everybody got ready.

Frieda came running over early on Sunday morning, waving a scrap of paper. "My permission slip," she said, taking charge at once. "You want permission slips from everybody, right? And I figured out about our ages. We have to be in the same grades as the kids in the letter-writing contest, okay?"

"Well, hey, I'm older than that," said Eleanor. "So is Robert."

"I mean from now on," said Frieda. "In case anybody else wants to come. And look, I've got a checklist of stuff we have to take. I've got this book at home. It all came out of the book. Here, I made five copies, one for everybody." Frieda licked her finger and handed them out efficiently.

Eddy looked at his copy warily. Frieda's list had a romantic ring, as if they were going on safari in Africa:

OFFICIAL CHECKLIST OF REQUIRED ITEMS
FOR BIVOUAC

permission slip	comb, washcloth, soap,
knapsack	small towel
sleeping bag	toothbrush, toothpaste
2 pairs comfortable shoes	money
3 pairs socks	flashlight
3 shirts	thermos
2 pairs shorts	sunburn lotion
1 pair long pants	Kleenex or toilet paper
3 underwear	stamped postcards ad-
1 heavy sweater or jacket	dressed to parents
1 sun hat with visor	first-aid kit for emergency
1 raincoat or poncho with	use in the field
hood	

Eddy snorted. "Where's the elephant gun?" he said. "How about medicine for snakebite?"

"Listen," said Frieda, "I already left out the compass and the emergency signal flares. I mean, I really pared it down."

In addition to the things on Frieda's list, everyone brought something extra. Eddy had a Frisbee and a radio. Eleanor had curlers, a pocket mirror and a pair of earrings. Frieda didn't have anything extra, but her sun hat was a pith helmet, and instead of a thermos she had a World War I Army canteen that had been handed down in the family. Robert had a butterfly net, a killing jar, a set of drawing pins, a flat box filled with cotton for mounting specimens, and a paperback book, *Butterflies and Moths of America.* Georgie had a book too, *Charlotte's Web,* even though she had read it thirteen times. And of course she carried her letter to the President, packed in the very bottom of her knapsack.

On Sunday they had to fend off Oliver Winslow. Oliver wanted to drive them to Washington in his car. But Eleanor put a stop to that.

"Listen, Oliver," she said firmly, "this is strictly a walking march. No cars, you hear? Especially that green horror of yours. No cars allowed. And anyway, you're too old. We've got this rule."

Uncle Freddy figured out how they were to go. He studied his road maps of New England and the Middle Atlantic seaboard, opening them out flat so that they overlapped.

"Here we are," he said, drawing his finger down in a curving line. "U.S. One. It goes all the way. It's the Boston Post Road, the old coach road to Providence and New York and Baltimore and Washington. You take Route One Twenty-six to Framingham, and Twenty-seven to Walpole, and pick up Route One there. Then you just stay on Route One the whole way. It isn't a big super-highway. It goes through little towns where you'll be able to buy food, towns where people are living. And you'll be able to find public phones so you can call us every day."

They were eager to get started. On Monday morning the five of them stood on the front porch with Aunt Alex and Uncle Freddy, anxious to finish their good-byes and get going. They were decked with backpacks and sleeping bags. Sweaters were knotted around their waists. Georgie's flag slanted back over her shoulder, rippling gaily in the light wind that was tossing the dewy sheets on the clothesline and lifting the birds on cushions of air.

"You're sure we can't drive you to Route One?" said Uncle Freddy. "It's a long way to Walpole. We could give you a good start."

"No, no," said Eleanor hastily. She looked at the others. "Is everybody ready?"

At last they were on their way. As they took their first strides on Walden Street, Eleanor glanced back over her shoulder, feeling already a twinge of homesickness. Uncle Freddy and Aunt Alex were still standing in front of the door, stiffly upright like the pillars of the porch.

"Good-bye," she shouted, waving her hand. The rest of them turned, too, and waved. Georgie's flag fluttered once as they went around the curve of the road, and then Aunt Alex and Uncle Freddy could see it no more. Georgie and her fellow marchers were gone.

"You know what she is, don't you?" said Uncle Freddy in melancholy understanding. "Georgie, I mean."

"What?" said Aunt Alex, looking at him sadly.

"A saint. Some new kind of saint."

Aunt Alex smiled. "That's what Miss Prawn thought, last fall, remember? She thought Georgie was a saint or a fairy of some kind."

"But it's true. She is a saint. That's what they're like. Through fire and torture and plague and the threat of death they do what they have to do. That's Georgie."

Aunt Alex uttered a hollow laugh. "I must say, I never thought about the parents of saints before, did you? I'll bet Joan of Arc's mother wished her daughter would just get married to the farmer next door and stay home and feed the chickens."

PART TWO

The Peace Missile will give us a first-strike capability of such awesome power that no enemy will ever again dare to threaten our safety. . . .

James R. Toby
President of the United States
The White House
Washington, D.C.

The Peace Missile might kill all the plants and animals in the world by mistake someday, and that would be terrible. . . .

Georgie Hall
Grade 4
Alcott School
Concord, Massachusetts

The Call of the
Open Road

— ☆ —

Walden Pond was on their way. They walked
quickly past it into the town of Lincoln. Striding
along in single file, swinging their arms, full of
their mission, they soon crossed the boundary
into Wayland, with Georgie's flag fluttering and
rippling and furling and unfurling at the front
of the line. The sun shone. They ate all of Frieda's
mother's date bars. They ate the little boxes of
raisins. Cars whizzed by them on the busy road.
At first each car was a whispering hum, then a
purr, then a buzz, and then a rubbery sheeting
of tires on asphalt, and then the sound swiftly fell
away as the car disappeared from sight. Bicyclists
pedaled past them briskly, bent over their handlebars. Joggers caught up with them, gasping, their
arms and legs pumping, and vanished quickly,
far ahead.

By nightfall, they were only in Saxonville, on the outskirts of Framingham.

Frieda was appalled. "My mother *shops* in Framingham," she said.

They finished their day's march at St. George's Church in Saxonville, right beside the road. Behind the church there was a little grassy place beside the parking lot where they could spread out their sleeping bags and eat the last of their sandwiches.

After supper Robert disappeared with his butterfly net. Eddy went with him. But before long Eddy was back.

"Where's Robert?" said Eleanor sharply.

"He's looking for a phone booth."

"A phone booth? Why didn't he call his mother when we called Aunt Alex, back in Wayland?"

"How should I know?" Eddy picked up his Frisbee and tossed it at Frieda. Frieda snatched at it and missed, and the Frisbee went whirling into the bushes. She shrieked happily and plunged after it. Soon they were standing in a circle in the parking lot, tossing it back and forth. Frieda and Georgie never seemed to be able to catch it. They were always missing it and running after it, squealing. Eddy and Eleanor were wickedly good. They threw it and caught it and threw it and caught it and threw it viciously back again. Then Robert showed up and they all went to bed.

For a while they lay in their sleeping bags while Eddy's radio rocked with noisy music. Then Eddy switched it off. Now they could hear the silky sound of the cars on the road. The cars no longer seemed like machines with gasoline engines. They were more like something natural, like big shiny beetles whirring in the dark. The moon was overhead, caved in at one side like a dented beach ball. The wind made a threshing sound in the leaves, a sighing that blended with the sighing of the cars.

Eleanor lay on her side, inhaling the scent of last summer's trip to Mount Wachusett, captured in the kapok of her sleeping bag. Through two layers of thick cloth she could feel Georgie's knees pushing into the backs of her legs. Eleanor was full of doubt.

Today she had discovered that walking was different from driving. When Aunt Alex drove them somewhere, they just sat patiently in the car for a few minutes while houses and trees and stores whisked past, and pretty soon they were where they wanted to be. But walking! Walking meant that you put one foot down, and then the other, and moved slowly, slowly past one point on the horizon, slowly enough to inspect every tree and bush and flower and weed and pebble along the way. *Plod, plod, plod.* Eleanor fell asleep thinking, *This is impossible. It's just so incredibly impossible.*

When she woke up, the moon was gone. A bright planet was nestled in the top of a tree. The sky was bright with dawn light. She was tired of lying on her left side, so she rolled over on her right, then jerked her head back in surprise.

Georgie was staring at her, her glowing eyes an inch from Eleanor's face. "Oh, Eleanor," whispered Georgie, "isn't this fun?"

They were all awake. They crawled out of their sleeping bags and rolled them up. They had gone to bed in their clothes, so they were already dressed. They were hollow and hungry for breakfast as they hitched themselves into their backpacks.

Georgie staggered as the weight of her knapsack came down on her scrawny shoulders. But she didn't complain. She reached for the flag, which she had planted firmly the night before in a tulip bed.

Frieda was looking at her narrowly. "Listen," she said, "you've got too much to carry." She looked around imperiously. "Now hear this," she said loudly, "from now on we'll take turns carrying the flag. I'll be the Flag Person for today, okay, Georgie?"

But Georgie wouldn't part with the flag. "It's not heavy," she said. "I can carry it all right."

Frieda gave up. It was the kind of small crisis that would be repeated over and over again on the long journey. They would bicker and argue, and then Georgie would murmur something, and the rest of them would look at each other and say, "Well, all right." It was Georgie's march, after all. Her high purpose was the reason for everything they did, for every step they took on the road. They didn't talk about it, but they felt it, every one of them, from the very beginning.

"Well, okay," said Frieda. She turned away and looked around for other worlds to conquer. (Frieda had been born a four-star general.) "I know," she said. "A Bag Person! We need a Bag Person to carry all our trash, so we don't litter the road. You know, candy wrappers and old Kleenexes, stuff like that. And whenever we come to a trash barrel, the Bag Person will throw it all away. I hereby appoint Robert Toby as Bag Person for today." Frieda pulled a plastic bag out of her knapsack and handed it to Robert with a lordly gesture.

"Oh," said Robert, looking at the bag in surprise. "Well, okay." He took the bag and stuck it in the top of his pants.

It was strange to be walking so early, at dawn, without any breakfast. They walked an hour before they found the Bumblebee Café. Sitting down at the counter, they felt like tramps. Their teeth were unbrushed. Their mouths felt queer. Their faces had not been washed. Their hair was uncombed. They took turns in the rest rooms, and tried to clean themselves up.

In the ladies' room Eleanor looked at herself in the mirror and knew she would never use the curlers she had packed in her knapsack in the first flush of excitement over the fact that Robert Toby was coming along. She pulled out the bag of curlers and put it down on the sink beside the faucet.

There was no point in trying to look nice for Robert Toby. Even though they were marching along practically side by side, Robert never spoke to Eleanor. He didn't talk to anybody but Eddy. He wasn't interested in girls. Maybe next year he would be different. Maybe then he would notice Eddy's sister for the first time. Eleanor imagined Robert meeting her in the hall outside Mr. Orth's French class and saying, "Hiya, baby, where have *you* been all my life?" She burst out laughing.

Georgie was in one of the compartments. She opened the door and stood in her socks and looked at Eleanor solemnly. "Come look," she said.

Eleanor went into the compartment. "Look at what?" she said.

"It's blue," said Georgie, pointing.

"So it is," said Eleanor, studying the blue water in the toilet. "Some kind of disinfectant, I guess."

"What's blue?" demanded Frieda, who was doing up her pigtails. She looked too, and then burst out laughing. "Blue!" And then Georgie laughed too, and then the two of them went into one of their giggling fits.

Eleanor shrugged, astonished at this new proof that she was so much older and more mature than anybody else on this march.

It took them two hours to get through the sprawling city of Framingham. The pancakes they had eaten for breakfast sank to the bottoms of their stomachs like stones. Turning onto Route 27, they trudged along without speaking, thinking only of their destination, Route 1, the shining path that was to be their constant companion, their king's highway, their royal road to Washington.

And then, three miles from Route 1, their

number suddenly increased. The five of them suddenly became seven.

"Wow," said Eddy, "an Alfa Romeo. Hey, look, it's stopping."

The Alfa Romeo was squealing to a sudden stop fifty yards ahead of them, pitching forward, then backing up.

"Watch out," said Frieda. "My mother said not to talk to strangers, especially in cars."

But there were no strangers in the Alfa Romeo. It was Cissie Updike's mother's car. Cissie was a sixth grader in the Sanborn School. Eddy knew her well. Her mother was jumping out of the car, reaching into the backseat, yanking something out, jerking it open, and setting it down beside the road. It was a baby stroller. Then, while Cissie opened the trunk and took out her backpack, her mother reached into the car again, plucked out a baby, and plopped it into the stroller. Then, before anyone could protest, Mrs. Updike kissed Cissie, kissed the baby, jumped back into the car, put her foot on the accelerator, sped away, screeched the car around in a wild U-turn, and then whizzed past them again, her skinny face white at the window. She was gone!

"My mother," said Cissie wearily. "Honestly, she's really bonkers."

Eleanor found her voice. "Listen," she gasped, "you can't bring that baby."

"A permission slip," spluttered Frieda. "I'll bet he hasn't got a permission slip."

"Yes, he does." Cissie pulled two pieces of paper out of her pocket and presented them to Frieda.

Eddy couldn't believe it. "But your mother, she's not letting you take the baby!"

"Oh, it was her idea," said Cissie airily. "But, really"—Cissie looked fondly at the baby—"he's really just incredibly good. I take care of him all the time at home."

Georgie bent down and cooed at the baby. "What's his name?" she said.

"Carrington. Carrington Chalmers Updike. He's fourteen months old."

They stood in a dumbfounded circle and gazed at Carrington Updike.

Carrington looked back at them, chuckling. He was a good-looking baby with fat red cheeks, smartly dressed in blue overalls and a microscopic pair of jogging sneakers.

Eddy waved his hands in helpless outrage. "Look, we can't take a baby on a long march like this. How will we ever get to Washington with a baby?"

But the baby had already won his case. The

rest of them were melting. Even Robert Toby was kneeling in front of Carrington, poking him in the stomach, making him laugh. Carrington's laughter was delicious, a deep throaty gurgling.

Eleanor couldn't understand how Cissie's mother could give up a baby like that, and send it out on the highway. Maybe she was some kind of horrible person who hated her children and wanted to get rid of them. "What about diapers?" Eleanor said feebly to Cissie. "You can't possibly have enough diapers for a whole trip to Washington."

"He doesn't wear diapers anymore," said Cissie triumphantly. "Carrington's amazing. He's a superbaby. He wears pants. He drinks from a cup. You'll see."

"How did you hear about us anyway? How did you know where to find us?"

"Oh, it's all over town. Frieda's mother told my mother, and your Aunt Alex called the school superintendent to explain why all you kids were going to be missing the rest of the term. You know what? I bet some more kids show up. You know, they're all"—Cissie watched a Hostess Cake van speed by them on the road—"worried too."

"But how did you know what to bring? I mean, we've got this list—"

"Oh, sure." Cissie recited the list glibly. "Three shirts, two pairs of shorts, flashlight, postcards, first-aid kit for emergency use in the field. Carrington and I, we've got everything. I think they're going to print the list in the paper."

They set off again, the seven of them, walking along Route 27 on the way to Walpole and Route 1. Cissie pushed Carrington's stroller. The little wheels chirped noisily, but they rolled easily over the bumpy ground.

It was crazy, it was insane, but it worked. Carrington Updike was the best thing that had happened to the march so far. He took to it immediately. It was as though he had spent a lifetime bounding along the road in a squeaking chariot. Carrington Updike had heard the call of the open road.

"P.S. Please, Mr. President . . ."

— ☆ —

On the broad landscape of New England they were only seven tiny dots creeping southward across eastern Massachusetts. Far away in Washington, D.C., the first of the fifty winners in the President's letter-writing contest was reading her letter aloud to the President in the Oval Office in the White House.

Susan Hobbs was a seventh-grade girl from Juneau, Alaska. Susan had been picked up in Juneau the day before by the President's private plane, Air Force One, and flown to Washington and settled comfortably in a guest room on the third floor of the White House.

Her letter was superb. Mrs. Goodspeed, the principal judge of the letter-writing contest, had pounced on it at once.

Susan held it in one hand while she gripped

the staff of the sparkling flag with the other. The dazzling sequins on the stars of the flag flashed in her eyes, making it difficult to read. But she knew her letter by heart.

"Dear Mr. President," recited Susan, "to me the flag of the United States stands for snow-capped mountains and cold blue rivers, and for salmon canneries on the shore of the Gulf of Alaska. . . ."

Susan's letter was about her own home state. For Susan, the most important thing about the American flag was the single star that represented Alaska.

When she was finished, the President congratulated her warmly.

"Oh, but I'm not finished," said Susan. "There's a P.S. at the end."

"Well, let's hear that too."

"P.S.," said Susan shakily, staring at the blank white space at the bottom of her letter. "Please, Mr. President, I hope you change your mind about the Peace Missile."

The postscript to Susan's letter was brand-new. It had not been okayed by Mrs. Goodspeed. Susan had made it up courageously at the last minute.

The President had not expected this mild attack. "Ah, well, my dear," he said kindly, "I don't think you should trouble your pretty little head about a thing like that. Now let's get to work, shall we? I've got to swear in a new member of my cabinet. Follow me, and hold those colors high."

The President and Susan Hobbs were not the only people hard at work in the White House that morning. In the east and west wings there were many other offices.

One was the office of the Department of Grass Roots Information. It was a small one-person compartment in the basement of the east wing. The Director of Grass Roots Information spent his days reading small-town newspapers, looking for stories about the President. Whenever he found something about President Toby, he cut it out and filed it away.

It was a boring job. On the day when the May 23rd issue of the *Concord Journal* landed on his desk, the Director of Grass Roots Information was almost asleep. He was so drowsy he almost missed the article about the children who were marching to Washington.

But then it caught his eye, and he woke up.

CONCORD KIDS MARCH TO WHITE HOUSE

said the small headline on page four.

The Director of Grass Roots Information picked

up the paper and took it down the hall to his boss in the White House Office of Public Relations.

The Public Relations Director read the tiny article, then tapped it with his finger. "Keep an eye on that," he said.

The Royal Road

— ☆ —

They stood beside U.S. 1, shocked and disappointed. The shining boulevard that was to take them all the way to their destination, the charming old road that had carried coach traffic to New York and Washington throughout American history, wasn't at all what they had expected.

"It's a strip," said Eleanor, indignant.

"A strip?" said Frieda. "What's that?"

"This kind of road," said Eleanor. "All those horrible big signs. Junk food places, big gas stations and discount stores, shopping malls. They don't allow this kind of stuff on the big interstate highways, so they put it on the smaller roads instead."

"This isn't a smaller road," said Cissie. "Look, it's four lanes wide."

"What's the matter with junk food?" said Eddy.

"Look, there's a Mister Donut. We could go there for lunch."

There was a hot discussion about where to have lunch. They were starved. They ended up in a Burger King.

As soon as they walked in the door there was a crisis.

The man at the counter took one look at them and shouted, "Hey, you kids, why aren't you in school?"

Eleanor gaped at him, at a loss for words. But Frieda piped right up. "We go to private school. We're all finished for the summer."

Georgie looked at her, amazed. "Well, it's true," whispered Frieda. "Concord Academy's all finished. So is Middlesex."

The man at the counter seemed satisfied. He lowered a basket of sliced potatoes into a pot of boiling fat and shouted an order to the woman in the kitchen.

They sat down at a plastic-topped table, all crowded in together. Cissie pulled Carrington's stroller up close. Lunch was delicious. They ate hamburgers and chocolate sundaes and French fries and milk shakes and Cokes and a lot of other things their parents would have frowned at. They were not with their parents. They were on their own, masters and mistresses of their own fate. Their spirits lifted. Once again they felt the sense of careless freedom they had tasted at the beginning.

But after lunch, making their first walking acquaintance with Route 1, they were dismayed.

In its present condition as a modern highway it was not meant for walking. It had been built for automobiles, for cars in a hurry, for drivers who wanted to pull up beside a fast-food place to gobble a snack, or pick up a bargain at a discount house, or trade in their old Pontiac for a new Toyota.

The side of the road was not like the grassy verge of Route 126. It was not a country lane where you could catch glimpses of lady-slippers blooming in the woods. The shoulder was weedy and hard packed, glittering with fragments of broken glass, littered with the things people throw out of cars, beer cans and whiskey bottles, unwanted pieces of clothing, fast-food containers and empty cigarette packages. And sometimes there were ominous things that seemed left over from some terrible accident—a single shoe, or the fragments of a blown inner tube. On the road itself there were wild curving lines of black, the traces of tires frantically seizing the road as some driver swerved and braked in the path of an appalling catastrophe.

Uncle Freddy had looked at the map and promised them little towns. Route 1 would go through towns where people were living, he had said. But there were no towns, no pleasant front yards and suburban cottages, only here and there a few houses that had been tortured into stores.

Georgie didn't care what the road was like. She picked her way around a broken chunk of asphalt and a huge rubber mudguard that had whipped off a passing truck, and looked back at Carrington, as he plunged after her in his stroller, strongly pushed by Robert Toby.

Carrington was as contented as ever. He smiled back at Georgie.

But Eleanor's doubts were riding high. She fell back to walk with Cissie. It was impossible to talk. Above the throbbing sound of the cars, the trucks made a heavier noise. The great steel rigs thundered past them with a roar, and above the roar there was a singing scream on one note. It was the shriek of the enormous tires on the metallic surface of the highway.

How could they stand it? wondered Eleanor in despair. How could they possibly endure it for six long weeks?

An Arrow Pointed South

— ☆ —

But the real trouble with the march to Washington was too many leaders.

Of course, Eleanor should have been the leader, because she was the oldest, and she had a naturally bossy disposition.

So did Cissie, as it turned out. Cissie was a very strong-minded girl.

Frieda, too, was born to command, and even though she was only in the fourth grade, she had an organizing kind of mind. She was always proposing rules for what she called the "pilgrimage"—rules about the sharing of duties, rules about important things like safety and health.

Eddy, too, had clear opinions, but Eddy's were mostly about his own behavior, things he felt like doing himself. He didn't want anyone else telling him what to do, especially Eleanor or Cissie or Frieda.

Everybody knew that the real leader of the march was Georgie. But Georgie's way of leading was not to lead at all. Georgie never told anybody what to do. She walked in the middle of the small procession, or at the front, or at the rear, carrying her flag. She never said "Now, listen everybody," like Frieda, or "Stop that," like Eleanor, or "I think that's really dumb," like Cissie, or "Why don't we eat now?" like Eddy. The only thing swelling in Georgie's heart was gratitude that the others had come along, and fear that they might weary of the whole thing and decide to go home.

She was glad to obey everybody's orders. She walked along easily, carrying her big pack without complaint. Whenever they stopped to rest, she played with Carrington, or leaned against a guardrail with her big flag, reading Robert's *Asterix* comic book, or stood still while Eleanor combed her hair and snapped the elastics on her ponytails.

Eleanor was keeping a watchful eye on Georgie. It was amazing that Georgie didn't get tired. Maybe there wasn't enough *to* her to get tired. Maybe she was like those birds that rested in the air, that never needed to come down. Her light bones carried no plump body weight. Her thin legs could just go stilting along forever. And her urgent desire to get to Washington was stronger, pushing her forward, than the heaviness of her backpack dragging her down. She was like an arrow pointed south.

The rest of them were aware of it, the southward aim of Georgie's arrow, the forward lean of her flag. That was why they went on walking among the discarded license plates and hubcaps, the cans and bottles, the broken glass, while the cars and trucks whizzed past them. They stumbled along in a clumsy line, wavering and pausing but still going, following the fluttering stars of Georgie's flag and the other star of her steadfast will.

Eddy and Robert invented a pastime—identifying cars. "Subaru!" shouted Eddy as the cars rushed by. "Chevy Caprice! Ford Mustang!"

"Thunderbird!" cried Robert. "Datsun! Oldsmobile Cutlass police cruiser! Uh-oh, look, the cruiser's slowing down."

Eddy and Robert glanced at each other, as the police cruiser pulled over in front of them and backed up.

"What does *he* want?" said Frieda.

A state trooper was getting out of the cruiser, walking heavily back to meet them. He was tall with a broad, expressionless face. His eyes were invisible behind his dark glasses.

He was polite. "Where do you kids think you're going?"

Eleanor opened her mouth, but couldn't speak. *Washington, D.C.,* sounded too silly in her head. Instinctively she looked at Georgie.

The others were looking at Georgie too. It was *her* march, after all.

But Georgie was gazing dreamily at the cars streaking past on the other side of the highway. She didn't say anything.

Eddy spoke up boldly. "We're on our way to Washington."

"We're not hitchhiking," said Frieda quickly. "We're just walking, and we've got permission slips from our parents."

"You're walking to Washington?" The police officer was stunned. "Washington, D.C.?"

They all nodded vigorously, Frieda and Eleanor and Georgie and Cissie and Eddy. Carrington felt the heightened excitement in the air, and clapped his hands. Eleanor looked around for Robert. Where was he?

The policeman was taking off his hat and rubbing his hair, which was red like Eddy's and Eleanor's. "But Washington is four hundred miles away. Maybe five hundred."

They all nodded again, agreeing eagerly. "You're right. That's right. We know."

"Look," he said, gesturing helplessly. And then words seemed to fail him. He blew out his cheeks.

"Is there any law against it?" said Frieda defiantly.

The policeman fell back on a formula. "Let me see those permission slips," he said gruffly.

Obediently they dropped their knapsacks on the ground and poked inside them. Eleanor had to take every single thing out of hers. At last she shook her heavy sweater and the permission slip fluttered out.

"Hmmm," said the policeman, stroking his chin, examining the permission slips and giving them back. "Well, listen here. Tell me, what do you want to go to Washington *for?*"

Again they all looked at Georgie, who saw with dismay that it was her turn at last. She stepped forward one step, and gripped the mop handle of her flag. It flapped idly forward, and brushed the policeman's blue clean-shaven jaw. "To see the President," whispered Georgie.

"What did you say, honey?" said the policeman, bending down.

Georgie cleared her throat and spoke louder. "To see the President."

"The President?" He couldn't believe his ears. "You kids want to talk to the President of the United States? What about?"

They all spoke at once, explaining, waving their hands.

"Okay, okay." He shook his head and gestured at them to quiet down.

"Look," said Frieda belligerently, "we're citizens of this country, right? Is there any law against citizens of the United States talking to the President of the United States?"

The policeman was stumped. He put his hat back on and took off his glasses and wiped them on his sleeve. His eyes looked tired. "No, I guess not," he said, and then he put his glasses back on and wheeled around and went back to his car.

Eleanor nudged Georgie. "Come on," she said.

Resolutely the marchers set their faces forward and walked ahead. Cissie gave the stroller a shove and Carrington's wheels went around again, squeaking cheerfully. Georgie's flag swelled out in a splendid display of stars and stripes. As the cruiser edged out onto the road, the police officer waved at them, and then his car picked up speed and shrank rapidly as he drove away in the direction of the Twin Lanterns Lounge and the Sunset View Motel and the Honda sales room and the Hai-Lua Chinese Polynesian restaurant.

But it wasn't the end of his interest in Georgie's march to Washington. A moment later two cruisers from the Foxboro Police Department caught up with them, their blue lights flashing, and slowed down.

"That guy, he must have called them on his radio," said Eddy.

"Just look straight ahead," hissed Eleanor. "Just keep going."

The two cruisers didn't stop. They merely drove along beside the procession at three miles an hour, while the drivers stared at the peculiar sight of a parade of children bound on a crazy journey.

It was hard to keep walking while being stared at. Eleanor stumbled over a dirty scrap of carpet and pitched forward.

Then an officer leaned out the window of one of the cruisers and waved to them. "Good luck," he said loudly. "I hope you make it to Washington."

Georgie was thrilled. She beamed at the policeman and waved her hand, as the two police cars picked up speed and drove away.

"Who's that?" said Frieda warily. A boy was climbing over the guardrail far ahead of them. He gestured at them nonchalantly with his butterfly net. It was Robert.

They looked at each other in surprise. No one had missed him but Eleanor. She called to him sharply, "Where were you?"

Robert walked up to them calmly. "I caught an Eastern Meadow Fritillary," he said. Reaching into his net, he brought out a small spotted butterfly and held it on his finger.

They gathered around and watched, as the Eastern Meadow Fritillary opened and closed its orange wings. Then Robert tossed it over his head. Miraculously the butterfly stood in the air for a moment, vibrating its wings, and then it fluttered up, higher and higher, until it vanished in the leaves of a half-dead tree.

"Why didn't you keep it?" said Eleanor, staring up at the tree.

"Oh, I've got plenty of those," said Robert.

There was a pause in the traffic on the road, and for a few seconds they all stood still, looking up. But then an empty flatbed truck went by with a bang and a rattle, and they remembered where they were and what they were doing, and they took deep breaths and started to walk again.

"Washington or bust, right?" said Eddy, grinning at Robert.

"Right," agreed Robert amiably. "Washington or bust."

Menace on the Road

— ☆ —

By five o'clock that afternoon they were exhausted. Carrington was asleep in his stroller, his head wobbling on his chest as the little wheels jounced and bounced on the pebbly shoulder of the highway.

"We've got to find a place to eat," said Frieda.

There were no fast-food drive-ins anywhere in sight, no Mister Donut, or McDonald's, or Kentucky Fried Chicken. All they could see ahead of them was a gas station with a towering sign that revolved on its tall pole, proclaiming GETTY to all points of the compass, and a huge brick building with letters mounted separately on the ridge of the roof, spelling L I Q U O R S. Far in the distance was a colossal shopping mall with acres of blacktop and great sprays of lights like bouquets of metal flowers. After the shopping mall

they walked past a stretch of devastated country-
side traversed by high-tension wires. And beyond
the high-tension wires crouched a restaurant called
the Pirate Cave.

"Hey, what about this place?" said Eddy. "Come
on."

Eleanor studied the Pirate Cave, then grabbed
Eddy's arm and pulled him back. "Not here, Eddy,"
she said, shuddering. The place was a sleazy-
looking roadhouse with dead evergreen plant-
ings, a broken door, and small dark windows with
plastic shutters. Hurriedly Eleanor bundled
Georgie past it, imagining sinister people within,
looking out at them with dull eyes, then coming
outdoors to snatch them inside.

It was a grim stretch of road. Before long
Eleanor was wishing for the protection of even
such a scary sanctuary as the Pirate Cave.

The parade of motorcycles was like something
Eddy had seen on television. They were big Su-
zukis and Harley Davidsons, custom superbikes,
stripped and chopped, gaudy with flashy paint
jobs. Their front wheels stuck way out forward.
Their riders lay in awkward postures with their
brawny bare arms stretching to the Ape-hanger
handlebars. Their helmets glittered in sparkling

colors. Their mirrored goggles covered half their faces.

They were going the other way, but when they saw the procession of children, they wheeled around in thunderous U-turns and headed back.

"Oh, no," whimpered Cissie. She snatched up Carrington, picked up the stroller, and scuttled along with the wheels banging against her side.

"Keep going," shouted Eddy above the backfiring explosions of the big choppers as they blatted slowly beside the seven children, their wheels weaving in and out. The first biker was keeping pace with Eleanor. Curly gray hair poured out from under his gold helmet. He grinned at her and pulled his bike dangerously close, crowding her against the guardrail. Terrified, Eleanor squeezed against the rail and threw out her hands to fend him off, her heart racing.

Then something happened. The bikers were looking back down the road. Then, all together, they turned back out on the highway, throttling up, jamming into low gear, taking off with an earthshaking multiple roar.

Only when they were gone did Eleanor hear the siren.

The police cruiser shrieked past them with a comforting *Wow-wow-wow-wow-wow*.

Was it pursuing their tormentors? They didn't care. They sank to the ground, gasping, letting out their suspended breath. Cissie put Carrington back in his stroller and fed him sips of milk from the cup on the top of her thermos. The rest of them sat silent and watched Carrington's lower lip wobble as he gulped the milk. Some of it dribbled down his chin. Cissie wiped him clean, and murmured, "Isn't it good, Carrington? Isn't it delicious?"

"Does he talk yet?" said Frieda curiously.

"No," said Cissie, "but he's really smart, you can tell."

"*I* talked when I was nine months old," said Frieda. "Does he walk?"

Cissie glowered at Frieda. "Not yet. I suppose you walked when you were born, right? You just got right up and walked out of the hospital, right?"

"No," laughed Frieda. "I just sat in my playpen until I was two. They thought there was something wrong with my legs. But there wasn't, see?" Frieda stood up and jigged clumsily for a second, and looked at Georgie, and Georgie burst out laughing, and then they all got up and walked on.

They were very tired. Their five minutes of fright had worn them out. In their weariness they kept stumbling over pieces of litter. They were walking through a jungle of liquor bottles and beer cans and limp paper bags. Somebody had emptied all the trash out of a car. Cigarette butts were scattered everywhere, and plastic six-pack loops and chunks of Styrofoam.

Bleakly Eleanor began to wonder why they bothered to go on. Maybe it wasn't worth it, the whole crazy trip. Maybe it was stupid to try to keep the earth from blowing up in some final disastrous nuclear explosion. Except for Concord, Massachusetts, the whole world was a pretty horrible place. Maybe it wasn't worth saving.

When another car pulled up beside them they were almost too worn out to care whether it was friend or foe.

A young woman was getting out. She seemed flustered. "Hey," she said, "are you the kids walking to Washington? You know, about whatsis, the Peace Missile?"

They all nodded, and looked at her blankly.

She was flourishing a camera. "Okay if I put you kids in the *Providence Journal*? Tomorrow morning's edition? I'm the police reporter. See, what I do is, I call up the desk sergeant and he tells me what's up. He got an item on you kids from Foxboro. Hey, move closer together, okay?

Wait a minute, that baby's real cute. Put the baby in the middle."

Obediently they huddled together while the reporter took their picture. Carrington chuckled and laughed for the camera. The rest of them stood listlessly.

"Thanks a heap," said the reporter. Running around her car, she climbed in and drove away.

Instantly Robert popped up again, ambling out from a scrawny stand of trees.

"Where were you this time?" said Eddy. "Butterflies again?"

But Robert merely shrugged his shoulders and mumbled, "Looking for a bathroom."

They all laughed, and Eddy made a joke. "You weren't looking for a bathroom, you were looking for a big tree."

A big tree. In their dog-tired state it was the funniest thing they had ever heard. Thereafter *big tree* was part of their language. It was a comical way of explaining why you had to disappear for a minute.

They were hungry as well as tired. "Now hear this," said Frieda grouchily. "If we don't find a place to eat pretty soon, I'm going to just really, you know, scream or something."

But it was two long miles before they found

the Silver Spoon. They didn't even bother to look at it closely. They didn't care what it was like. They were starved.

Inside, the Silver Spoon was more like a noisy cocktail lounge than a restaurant. They sat in a dingy booth and had Cokes and expensive snacks. They ate hungrily. The jukebox crashed and howled.

Robert finished first, and slid off the bench. "Got to call my mother," he said. Eddy got up too, and fished in his pocket for quarters.

"Oh, well, never mind," said Robert quickly, sitting down again. "You go first."

"Well, okay," said Eddy. Later on, coming out of the men's room, he passed Robert at the telephone.

Robert was hunched up against it, talking to his mother. "What noise? Oh, that? Oh, it's just the traffic on Pennsylvania Avenue, and I guess they're having a party in the—ah—Blue Room."

What was that all about? Puzzled, Eddy sat down in the booth again, as Cissie got up. "I'm going to give Carrington a sponge bath," she said, heading for the ladies' room, lugging her little brother.

But a moment later she was back. "Ugh," she said. "I'll wait till we find a nice clean gas station. He'll just have to go to bed dirty." Cissie looked

anxious. "Hey, where are we going to sleep anyway?"

They stood outside the Silver Spoon, staring
down the road. It was too dark to see.

"We promised Aunt Alex we wouldn't walk in
the dark," said Eleanor.

"Anyway," complained Frieda, "I can't walk
another step."

Hesitantly they explored the dim spaces behind the Silver Spoon. The parking lot stretched
to the edge of a swampy hollow. Below them they
could see scummy surfaces, little pools of stag-
nant water. Beside them a big dumpster loomed
on the pavement, overflowing with trash bags and
loose garbage. But beyond the swamp in the fad-
ing light they could make out misty blurs of trees,
decked in the tremulous pale green of the woods
in May. And far away behind the trees there were
the lighted windows of houses. There would be
kids in the houses, probably, and mothers and
fathers, and beds with soft pillows and blankets
and nice clean sheets.

They didn't know what else to do. Doubtfully
they unstrapped their sleeping bags and laid them
out on the compacted dirt between the pavement
and the swamp. Then they crawled into them and
tried to go to sleep.

Cissie and Carrington were snuggled in the same sleeping bag. Cissie held the baby close against her cheek, sniffling a little. The march to Washington wasn't what Cissie had expected.

It wasn't what the others had expected either. They lay in the glare of the spotlight at the back door of the Silver Spoon, trying to get used to the perpetual roar of the cars on the road. It was as though they were lying directly in the stream of traffic. And whenever there was a lull in the steady whine of gasoline engines, they could hear rustlings in the dumpster, as if rats were moving around inside, feasting on scraps of bologna sandwiches and taco chips and puddles of ice cream. The jukebox in the Silver Spoon thumped and hollered, and around their faces the mosquitoes gathered in clouds.

It was impossible. Groaning, they stumbled to their feet and bundled up their sleeping bags and struggled down the road in the direction of nowhere, limping in a wavering line, hugging the guardrail, turning pale faces away from the blinding flash of headlights.

But then their luck changed. They came upon a side road. Without a word, they turned into it and found themselves stumbling along beside a fence. On the other side of the fence there was a sense of openness and space. It was a field. Not just a field, a pasture.

"Look," whispered Georgie. "Horses."

There they were, dim and huge, two horses standing nose to tail. As Cissie handed Carrington over the fence to Robert, the horses lifted their heads and made soft whinnying sounds.

Gratefully Eleanor crawled once again into her sleeping bag and lay still, hearing only the distant drone of the highway and the snuffling breath of the great animals nearby. Grinding her feet into the bottom of the bag, she crowded up against Georgie, feeling around her the pure dark sky and the grassy field. Drifting off to sleep, she twisted her fingers in the hem of Georgie's flag and floated westward over the continent. Below her there were bright towns and cities and the broad outlines of farmers' fields and the dark shapes of wrinkled mountain ranges. The country was worth preserving after all, dreamed Eleanor, and she was glad. It was something she had today begun to doubt.

The March Becomes
a Crusade

— ☆ —

Eleanor opened her eyes to see Georgie's legs bobbing up and down beside her. Georgie was up and ready to go, as though she had heard a trumpet call at dawn, *tarantara!* She was standing patiently beside Eleanor, waiting for Eleanor to wake up. Her pack was on her back, her flag was in her hand.

Eleanor groaned and closed her eyes. But soon they were all up and about, moving around sleepily. In the light of day the pasture was a brilliant green, and the horses, brown and black, stood steaming in the cool morning air. There were apple trees in blossom and a white ramshackle barn and a farmhouse with carved fretwork on the porch. Behind the house, laundry hung on a line stretched between two poles. Eleanor had a sudden vision of Aunt Alex with clothespins in her mouth, and she felt a tug of homesickness.

Reluctantly they left the field and the horses, and walked back to Route 1. After the sweetness of the farm it seemed dingier than ever. Frieda tripped on a piece of metal strapping. Eddy kept dodging a torn election poster, ELECT JERRY HERBY. It kept flapping up against the backs of his legs and clinging to him, urging him to ELECT JERRY HERBY, ELECT JERRY HERBY. At last he picked it up and threw it behind him. Instantly it flattened itself against Robert's sweater.

Robert laughed. "I don't want to vote for him either," he said.

They ate breakfast at a counter in an enormous Zayre's discount store, and cleaned themselves up in the rest rooms, struggling into clean clothes in the small compartments. Carrington had his bath.

"Well, sort of a bath," said Cissie, settling him once again in his stroller. Carrington smiled and gurgled, careless of being clean or dirty. Actually he looked fine. He was pink cheeked and more or less spotless in a pair of denim overalls.

"Okay if I push him?" said Eleanor.

"Of course," said Cissie. "Be my guest."

The third day's march was like the second. Except for a few stretches of pine woods and a single miraculous vision of a pond with water lilies, their journey was a seedy progress past automobile salesrooms and used-car lots, a mattress outlet, a McDonald's restaurant, a Taco Bell, a car wash, a carpet company, a package store, and a place that offered video entertainment and GoKart rides. The traffic was just as loud and fast and heedless as the day before.

In the afternoon it began to rain a little. It was just a light misting in the air. They stopped and pulled their ponchos and raincoats out of their packs. Cissie zipped Carrington into his snowsuit and snapped the hood tightly under his chin.

Georgie looked up anxiously at her flag. She was pleased to see that the rain was merely lying on it in beaded drops. The fabric wasn't going to be soaked through. She reminded herself that the cloth of the flag was made from the fleece of sheep, and sheep had to stay outdoors in all kinds of weather. She let the flag fly. It flapped ahead of her, then fell back and wreathed itself around her as if to shield her from the rain.

The day passed slowly. They put their feet down on the muddy ground and tramped on patiently, *plod, plod, plod*. The rain made their faces red and their fingers numb. Once again Eddy and Robert studied the cars on the road and tried to beat each other to the draw, shouting "Buick Riviera," "Chevy Malibu," "Dodge Dart," "Honda Accord," "Plymouth Reliant," and once—Robert gasped and grabbed Eddy's arm—"Rolls-Royce Silver Ghost."

Late in the afternoon they crossed the state line between Massachusetts and Rhode Island. Proudly they stood beside the sign *ENTERING RHODE ISLAND,* and grinned at each other and congratulated themselves and shook hands.

"Now we've only got Rhode Island and Connecticut and New York City to get through," said Frieda.

"And New Jersey and Maryland," said Eddy.

"And Pennsylvania," said Eleanor, her voice hollow. "Don't forget Pennsylvania."

They looked at each other, dismayed. It sounded terrible. All those states! They had been on the road so long already, and they had put only one state behind them. There were so many more!

Georgie looked at the others fearfully. Were they about to give up? Would she have to go on by herself?

But then Frieda began to laugh. And suddenly the whole thing seemed funny. What a crazy trip! It was really *crazy,* what they were doing. They stood laughing beside the Rhode Island sign, leaning over to poke Carrington in the stomach, to make him laugh too.

The first city in Rhode Island was Pawtucket. And on the outskirts of Pawtucket there was a surprise.

A Rhode Island State Police cruiser was waiting for them, pulled up beside the road across their path. As they came near, the police officer leaned toward them and made a huge beckoning gesture with his arm. "Follow me," he shouted. Then he drove slowly in front of them on the shoulder of Route 1.

"Maybe he's taking us to jail," said Eddy. He was only half joking.

Eleanor looked nervously at Frieda, but there didn't seem to be anything else for them to do. Reluctantly they followed in the wake of the cruiser as it slowed down and stopped beside a big wooden church.

There was a sign in front of the church:

THE EPISCOPAL CHURCH
OF THE ADVENT
PAWTUCKET, R.I.

Eddy nudged Eleanor and pointed to a poster that had been thumbtacked to the wooden frame of the sign:

WELCOME
CHILDREN'S
CRUSADE!

"Is that us?" said Cissie, excited. "Do you think they mean us?"

"We're not a crusade," said Frieda indignantly. "We're a pilgrimage."

"What's a crusade?" said Georgie.

"Well, it's just like a pilgrimage," said Eleanor doubtfully.

"Hey, where's Robert?" said Eddy, looking around. "He's gone again."

The state trooper was opening the door of the parish hall, turning to grin at them and welcome them inside.

And there in the parish hall of the Church of the Advent, in the church kitchen, they found another welcoming committee. It was six motherly-looking women in aprons, hurrying to heat up a big pot of spaghetti and set it on the table, pulling hot muffin tins out of the oven, dropping them on top of the stove.

Soon Georgie and Eleanor and Eddy and Cissie and Frieda were shoveling spaghetti onto their paper plates. The policeman chucked Carrington under the chin and said good-bye. Eleanor was astonished to discover how hungry she was for home-cooked food. She didn't look up from her plate until she had eaten everything. Then, passing it for more, she saw Robert Toby calmly helping himself to a blueberry muffin at the other end of the table. Had he been looking for butterflies again? There was no way of knowing with Robert.

"Oh, this is so delicious," said Eleanor, turning gratefully to the woman who was putting another pot of spaghetti on the table. She was a large middle-aged woman in a green apron. There was a funny message printed on her apron, *God loves the Irish.* "How did you know we were coming?" said Eleanor.

"It was in the paper this morning," said the woman. "Have another muffin? Be sure and save room for the butterscotch pie." Then she clasped her freckled hands and sat down beside Eleanor. "Listen, dear, I think you kids are great. My kids think so too. In fact they wanted to come with me this evening, but I left them home. I was afraid they'd want to join you. Because—you know—they're scared too."

Eleanor was astounded. "But why don't you let them come with us?"

"Oh, but it's so dangerous." The woman looked

shocked. "I mean, what you're doing. Marching so far. I mean, it's so far!"

Frieda leaned across the table to Eleanor, grinning happily. "They've invited us to sleep here, right inside the parish hall. Isn't that great?"

"And we're serving breakfast in the morning," said the woman in the green apron cheerfully. "French toast and maple syrup. Oh, that baby's so cunning." She reached out her arms to take her turn, as Carrington was passed from one motherly embrace to another. "Are you sure you won't let me take this baby home?"

After the wretchedness and discomfort of the Silver Spoon the night before, the hospitality of the Church of the Advent and the cozy softness of its sofa cushions and the cleanliness of its bathroom were a wonderful relief.

They couldn't stop grinning at each other as they lay down in their sleeping bags on the rug.

"What's that nice smell?" said Eddy, basking in warmth and comfort, sniffing the air.

"Incense," said Cissie, inhaling luxuriously.

The lovely smell of holiness surrounded them as they fell asleep. Only Eleanor lay awake, thinking uneasily about the first Children's Crusade. They had been holy, too, all those children. The Children's Crusade had happened hundreds of years ago, back in the Middle Ages, when Christian knights were traveling to Jerusalem to try to win it back from the Mohammedans. All those thousands and thousands of children had decided to go too. Only they never got as far as the Holy Land. Why not?

Eleanor lay drowsily on her back and looked up at Georgie's flag. The flag was leaning against a window, glowing brightly because a streetlight was shining through the glass.

Then she remembered what had happened, way back in the Middle Ages, and she sat up, jolted awake. The Children's Crusade had never made it to the Holy Land because they had been captured and sold into slavery. All those thousands and thousands of children!

Another Postscript for the President

— ☆ —

In the White House, a new winner in the letter-writing contest had taken over from Susan Hobbs, the girl from Alaska. The new flag bearer was from Tallulah, Louisiana. His name was DuBose Boudreau.

His first day on the job was Memorial Day. Therefore DuBose's first duty was to hold the Presidential flag while the President reviewed a company of Marines on parade on Pennsylvania Avenue.

DuBose stood stiffly beside the President, trying to keep his face as expressionless as the faces of the Marines, who were all marching at attention, staring straight ahead as if they were made of wood rather than flesh and blood, as if the most important person in the country were not looking down at them.

The flag hung stiffly too. It didn't lift and flutter, even though the day was breezy. The glittering sparkles had been glued so thickly to the cloth that it could no longer respond to the light pressure of the wind.

After the parade the President and DuBose went back to the Oval Office, and the President invited DuBose to sit on one of the white sofas and read his letter aloud.

DuBose was glad to oblige. He tugged his letter out of his pocket and began reading at once. "To me," read DuBose, "the American flag stands for the great Mississippi River, which runs past my house in Tallulah, Louisiana. Whenever I look at the flag I hear the tooting of the boats that go up and down the river between Vicksburg and New Orleans. And I think of Mark Twain's Huckleberry Finn, who tried to free his friend Jim from slavery by drifting down the river on a raft. . . ."

It was easy to see why DuBose's letter had been chosen by Mrs. Goodspeed's committee. The President congratulated him warmly.

"Oh, sir," said DuBose, speaking up bravely, "there's something I left out. I forgot to say how the flag stands for being friendly to other people. You know, like it says in the Bible."

"Of course, DuBose, of course," said the President.

"So maybe we shouldn't put that missile up there in outer space, right?"

"Now, see here, DuBose," said the President in surprise, "maybe you should just stick to the wonders of Louisiana. Your letter was just fine the way it was. Now, shall we go to the tea party?"

"Well, okay," said DuBose. Together they walked from the west wing to the Green Room, where the President's wife was entertaining the wives of the cabinet members. The First Lady made a fuss over DuBose and introduced him to her guests, and then the wives made a fuss over him too.

"Good-bye for now, DuBose," said the President. Smiling at the cabinet wives, he turned away and went back to the Oval Office.

His Personal Advisor, Charley Chase, was waiting for him, "Sir, I think you're going to have to do something about the rising tide of complaint from the country about the Peace Missile. I've been talking to the Deputy Press Secretary. He's going out of his mind. All those big correspondents are after him, asking what you think about all the protests. The mail is piling up, and it's all angry. The White House has never received so much mail, never in all history. And Congress! They're battering down my door. I've got senators and congressmen climbing in the window, so to speak."

The President was a man of decision. "Well, then," he said, "maybe it's time to make another television address to the nation. Look, Charley, you arrange it with the networks for tomorrow night. Make sure it's prime time. In the meanwhile, I'll get busy and work up an outline. Then I'll sit down with Mrs. Colefax and whip the speech into shape."

"Right, sir." Charley Chase departed, and the President sat down beside the fireplace with a pad of paper on his lap. He always found it easy to write a speech. He never had any trouble deciding what to say. And this afternoon he had been truly inspired by the stalwart Marines he had been reviewing, and by DuBose's delightful letter about Louisiana. It was refreshing to see the United States through the eyes of these young people, to see it as they saw it, rich with local history, studded with geographical splendors.

Soon the President was composing sentences about the Marines, and about DuBose Boudreau and Susan Hobbs. He would ask Mrs. Colefax to supply him with copies of their letters, so that he could quote some of the passages that showed so clearly what the flag of their country meant to them. Then it occurred to the President that he might include in his own speech an explanation of just what the flag meant to *him*, to him personally.

A personal confession about the flag would lead directly into a serious discussion of the importance of the Peace Missile. The President turned it over in his mind. What, exactly, *did* the flag mean to him?

Instantly pictures rushed into his head.

The young faces of the Marines, firm and controlled, as they marched like clockwork in parade formation . . .

His devoted generals, their service medals flashing as they stood saluting the Marines under the snapping flag with its bright streamers of red and white . . .

The Statue of Liberty holding up her torch as if she were guarding the American shore against enemies at every hand . . .

The brave fleet of nuclear submarines patrolling the waters, alert for trouble . . .

Tight squadrons of fighter planes thundering overhead, splitting the sky over Arizona and Michigan and Kansas and California, ready for action . . .

The new missile, nearly ready to be transported to the air base in Nevada, soon to be aloft in the starry sky, circling the earth, looking down at the enemies of America, ready to spot preparations for war, ready to attack, to annihilate, to win.

It was a glorious country, a nation secure against

the foe, brave in battle, pugnacious and strong. He was proud to be its President.

In the basement of the east wing, the Director of Grass Roots Information was far from the splendid halls and stately rooms occupied by the President. But he was aware of the President all the time, just the same. It was an honor to be working in the same complex of buildings as the most important person in the United States.

This afternoon, as usual, he was keeping an eye on the local newspapers of the fifty states. When he picked up the *Providence Journal*, he noticed the picture right away, the photograph of a flock of mournful-looking children. There was a heading, CHILDREN'S ANTI-NUKE CRUSADE.

It was the same bunch, decided the Director of Grass Roots Information. It was the same kids who had set out from Concord, Massachusetts, a few days ago.

Leaning back in his chair he studied the picture carefully. Then he threw back his head and laughed. They were marching with a baby. They wouldn't get far. Look at them! After three days on the road they weren't even in Providence, Rhode Island. (Providence just happened to be the home town of the Director of Grass Roots Information.) They still had hundreds and hundreds of miles to go. They'd never make it.

Still, he would keep the picture in his file. Snipping it out carefully, he tucked it into a folder with the earlier story from the *Concord Journal*. Then he took a paper bag out of his desk drawer and went outdoors to eat lunch in the dappled shade of a grove of oak trees beside the east wing.

The leaves on the oak trees were still very small. The Director of Grass Roots Information looked up at them and remembered a saying from his boyhood, *Plant corn when the oak leaves are the size of a mouse's ear.*

Well, that was what they would be doing, he reflected, back home on that little hardscrabble farm in Rhode Island where he had grown up. They'd be hilling up the corn.

Bingo, Carrington!

— ☆ —

But the Children's Crusade saw no one planting corn in Rhode Island. They weren't in farming country at all. They were lost in the city of Providence. The signs for Route 1 kept petering out, leaving them stranded on back streets that went nowhere. Kindly people sent them on wild goose chases in the wrong direction.

Providence was a big city. They began to think they would never find a way out. Again and again they went around the Rhode Island Capitol with its gleaming white dome, only to find themselves at the same construction site in the middle of town. Again and again they had to cover their ears to shut out the gigantic *chuff CRASH chuff CRASH chuff CRASH* of the pile driver.

And therefore they couldn't locate the Y.W.C.A. where they were supposed to eat a festive lunch, according to the ladies of the Church of the Advent

in Pawtucket, who had called ahead and arranged
the whole thing. By late afternoon they finally
found Route 1 again, but they were far from the
private school where they had been invited to
spend the night.

"How about this place?" said Eleanor wearily,
stopping in front of a stone building. It was a
small Catholic church. In the front yard there
was a big white statue of Jesus, and a sign, *BINGO
EVERY FRIDAY.*

"It looks okay to me," said Cissie.

The church was closed. There was no one to
talk to, to ask if it was all right. They found a
sheltered place beside the back door, out of sight
of the street, and slung down their backpacks. It
was a relief to take them off. The backpacks always felt heaviest at night, even though they had
abandoned things here and there to lighten the
burden. Eddy's radio had been left in a men's
room in a Texaco station in North Attleboro. At
a Mobil station in Pawtucket Georgie had walked
tearfully away from her precious copy of *Charlotte's Web.* Robert had given up his *Asterix* comic
book at a soft ice cream stand in Plainville.

"I wish we could go inside the church and wash
up," said Cissie, undoing her bedroll with sticky
fingers. She dabbed at the chocolate ice cream on
Carrington's face, the last remains of supper. All

night long, bundled up beside him in her sleeping bag, she could taste it on his fat cheek.

In the morning they were awakened by an astonished priest with a jug of flowers in his hand. He was about to open the church for early Mass.

"Good heavens," he said, "do you mean to tell me you children have been here all night?"

They sat up, tousled and sleepy, and Frieda tried to explain.

"But you could have spent the night indoors, if I'd only known," said the priest, and then he opened the church and let them use his private bathroom. One by one they washed as well as they could, trying not to splash the priest's white surplice hanging on the wall.

When they gathered on the front lawn to say good-bye, the priest was suddenly struck by an idea. "Wait a minute," he said, rushing up the steps into the church. In a moment he came down the steps again, carrying an enormous stuffed panda. "It's one of our bingo prizes," he said, handing it to Carrington.

"Bingo, Carrington!" laughed Eddy.

Carrington was overjoyed. He clasped the stuffed panda, disappearing behind its monstrous plushiness.

"Let's call it Bingo," said Cissie, stroking the

cheap fur. "Is that okay with you, Carrington? *Bingo*, Carrington. His name is *Bingo*. Isn't he cute, Carrington? Don't you just love Bingo? Say thank you to the nice man, Carrington."

Carrington obediently chuckled deliciously and waved bye-bye.

"You're welcome, I'm sure," said the priest with a broad smile.

That morning they found their way out of Providence at last. South of the city, Route 1 returned to its customary ugliness, to the automobile sales rooms and the cutely sinister cocktail lounges and the towering Getty signs and the enormous shopping malls covered with blacktop. It was as though they had gone around in a circle.

And the motorcycles were back on the road.

"Hide," cried Eleanor, hearing the thunder of the heavy bikes behind them.

But there was no place to hide. Once again Cissie jerked Carrington out of his stroller. This time she had to lug Bingo too. "I'll take Bingo," said Georgie. She ran along beside Cissie, carrying the stuffed panda, her flag dipping over her shoulder. Robert reached down and picked up a long chromium-plated piece of automobile bumper, left over from some smashup.

Once again the big bikes slowed down beside them, weaving crazily on the road.

"What you got in those backpacks?" said Gold Helmet.

"They got lotsa money, I bet," said Green Helmet.

"How much you got, Red?" said Purple Helmet, slowing his bike, walking it beside Eleanor, his black boots gripping the road.

But then, once again, the man with the gold helmet and the cascade of gray curls waved his arm and gestured them back out on the highway. He jerked his thumb at the traffic. "Commuters," he bawled. "Forget it."

Something flew high in the air and landed on Eleanor's shoe. It was a beer can, spouting beer. Shaking, enraged and frightened, she kicked it away, as the big choppers leaned sideways and blatted out onto the highway.

"Are you okay?" said Robert, looking at her soberly. He was still holding his heavy chunk of automobile bumper.

"Oh, sure." Eleanor swallowed hard. "I mean, I guess so."

Once again they had to stop to catch their breath. "Listen," said Frieda, her voice unsteady, "don't anybody mention this, next time you call your mother."

The Jaguar and the Hitchhiker

—☆—

The next stretch of road was different. It was free of fast-food drive-ins and second-hand car dealers and shopping plazas. Looking ahead, Eleanor saw the sky rise clear and pure over the rigid gritty surface of the road. On the horizon there were clouds the shape of fantastic countries she had imagined long ago when she was young.

Georgie walked at the head of the line, carrying her flag. It fluttered and curled and quivered as if it were playing with the air. The colors had been freshened by their exposure to sun and rain. The charred edges had been worn away, or else they had somehow healed themselves. They were ragged, but clean and bright. The stars were still uncountable. Cissie had tried to count them, and given up. So had Frieda. Robert had tried, only to find himself surrounded by a blizzard of white Cabbage Butterflies.

Robert and Eddy had made a game out of their pastime of identifying automobiles. They hiked along the road, shouting the names of cars that sped past them, adding up their scores. Ordinary cars like Buick Skylarks and Oldsmobile Omegas were worth one point. Anything out of the ordinary, like a Mercedes Benz or a Cadillac Seville, was worth five. All the northbound cars were Robert's, the southbound cars were Eddy's. They were always arguing what some car or other was worth, especially after Robert demanded fifty points when a splendid 1923 Auburn touring car rolled majestically down his side of the road.

"Dodge Aspen," muttered Eddy. "That's sixteen. Ford Mustang, seventeen. Another Aspen, eighteen."

"Hey," said Robert. "Brand-new Volvo. Five points, right?"

Eddy was chagrined. All the fanciest cars were on Robert's side. And then another fantastic piece of luck came Robert's way in the shape of a Karmann Ghia. "Fifty points," cried Robert. "That's a hundred and thirty-five altogether."

Eddy disagreed. The game threatened to break up in furious argument.

"Look, you dummies," said Frieda, "why don't you pay attention? Look what's parked right up ahead."

Robert and Eddy looked, and gasped, and stopped their bickering. It was the most beautiful car either of them had ever seen, a Jaguar XJS, a long, low, gleaming black sports car.

They crowded around it, admiring its mirror polish and shining curves.

But the driver was lowering the window, frowning at them. "Don't touch!" he said. "Don't any of you kids touch this car. This here is a very valuable car."

Eddy had been about to run his hand along the swollen flare of the fender. "Well, okay," he said, withdrawing his hand. "I guess you don't want any fingerprints on the paint job, right?"

"Darn right I don't." The owner was a timid-looking man with a few strands of gray hair slicked across his bald head. He was wearing a youthful blazer with gold buttons, a watermelon-pink shirt and a loud tie. "I'm just resting her," he said nervously. "I just picked her up in Providence. She's got to be broke in easy."

"She sure is a beauty," said Eddy admiringly.

The man seemed pleased. He didn't object when Eddy bent down and leaned his elbow carefully on the window to look in. Soon the bald-headed man was demonstrating all the features of the interior—the walnut veneer, the leather uphol-stery, the stereo speakers, the tape deck, the gauges, the tachometer, the speedometer that registered speeds as fast as one hundred and eighty miles an hour.

"V-twelve fuel-injected engine?" said Eddy knowingly.

"That's correct." Then the owner of the Jaguar sat up with a jerk. "What was that?"

"What was what?" said Eddy. "I didn't hear anything."

"A bump. I heard a bump." The bald-headed man opened the door of his car and struggled up from the low-slung seat. "What was that noise?" he said, staring angrily at Frieda and Georgie and Eleanor and Robert and Cissie and Carrington. "I heard a thump. Something crashed into the side of this here car."

Cissie looked guilty. "It was me, I guess. I mean it was the stroller. I picked up the baby and then the stroller sort of rolled into the car. I don't think it hurt the paint or anything. I mean, look, it's just a little tiny—"

The man was furious. His pasty face flushed with rage. He stalked around the car and stared at the stroller, which was resting gently against the glittering black rear fender, buffered by Bingo, Carrington's enormous stuffed panda.

"How do you know it didn't hurt it?" shrieked

the man, glaring at the fender. With shaking fingers he took his glasses out of his pocket, unfolded them onto his nose, and bent down to examine the fender. "Just because you don't see no scratch," he said, gazing around at Cissie angrily, "that don't mean there's no damage to the undercoat. You know, a flaw in the bonding down underneath there. I mean, thirty-five thousand dollars I paid for this car, and the first thing that happens is a bunch of juvenile delinquents come along and chip the paint. Get away from my car." He made shooing motions with his hand, as if the Children's Crusade were a flock of chickens. "Go on, get away."

"Well, *okay*," said Cissie. "All *right*."

They backed away, and the owner of the Jaguar marched around his car and got in again. He started the engine.

"Listen to it purr," muttered Robert, admiring the car in spite of himself.

The Jaguar moved away from them, going extremely slowly. Even out on the highway it didn't speed up. It crept along the road at twenty miles an hour.

Eleanor stared after it in surprise. "I thought those cars were supposed to go really fast," she said.

"Oh, sure," said Eddy. "But this guy is a real fruitcake. He thinks you have to take it easy with a brand-new engine." He grinned at Robert, as the Jaguar crept along Route 1. "But he doesn't need to take it *that* easy. Hey, Robert, you'll notice he's going south. Fifty points for me, right?"

"Oh, sure, sure," said Robert, waving his hand.

"Well, if you want to know what I think," said Frieda scornfully, staring after the Jaguar, "I think that man is just bananas. He's just too wrapped up in himself and his thirty-five-thousand-dollar car to think about anything else in the world."

"Not even the world itself," said Georgie, making a solemn joke.

They looked at her in surprise, while the joke spread to the horizon and bounced off the sky. Then they picked up their knapsacks and started along the sandy shoulder of Route 1, remembering their distant destination.

Almost at once they ran into Oliver Winslow.

They came over a low rise to see him holding out his thumb beside the highway. He was hitchhiking. Oliver caught sight of them at the same time, and he ran toward them, whooping.

They crowded around him, grinning and clapping him on the back. Even Eleanor was glad to see Oliver. Eddy grabbed him and danced him up and down. "Hey, Oliver, what are you doing here? Why didn't you drive your car?"

Oliver took off his hat and fanned his face. "Long story," he said. "I started this morning, filled her up, took off. Everything in A-one shape. Then she stopped cold on me just now, back there at the bus stop. *KABANG, KAPOW,* you shoulda heard it. Timing chain's busted. This kid at the gas station, he says, no, he doesn't sell parts, I gotta go to North Kingstown, get a new part. Only then this policeman comes along, big deal, says I can't leave without I pay a big fine, parking at a bus stop. You should see this cop, stuffed shirt, fancy uniform. He'll be back in an hour, he says, arrest me if my car's still there. Jeez, what could I do? Gotta get a new part. Hey, excuse me, I gotta get a ride." Oliver leaned way out into the road as two gleaming new cars whizzed past them. "Hey, *STOP*," yelled Oliver. He shook his head and put his hat back on and stuck his thumb out again. "It's no use. That kind of car never stops. It's usually some beat-up old boat that picks up guys like me. There, see? Look at that! See that?"

Oliver ran down the road as a pickup truck with a crumpled fender slowed down and stopped. "See you later," he yelled as he climbed in.

They watched as the pickup bounced back on

the road and took off, heading for North Kingstown. "What did he mean, 'See you later'?" said Eleanor. "He's not joining the crusade, is he?"

"I don't know," said Eddy. "Hey, listen, you hear that?"

They could all hear the *wow-wow* of the police siren. A long black official-looking car was pulling up beside them. It was covered with flashing lights. Georgie looked disapprovingly at the two new glittering presidential flags flapping on the fenders. She held the staff of her own flag tightly. Cissie picked up Carrington and held him close. Frieda backed up warily. "I'll bet it's Oliver's cop," said Robert dryly.

The police officer was looking at them, frowning. His chief's hat was stiff with gold braid. He stared inquisitively at Eddy. He inspected the baby. He glowered at Georgie's flag. But he had something else on his mind. "You kids seen a hitchhiker here anywheres?"

There was a pause. Then Eddy spoke up thoughtfully. "What kind of hitchhiker do you mean?"

"Oh, you know. Big ratty-looking kid. Lotta hair."

"Oh," said Eddy, his face lighting up as if the truth were dawning. "He had this funny hat, right?

And one gold earring, right? Oh, him! Oh, sure, we saw him get a ride just a little while ago."

"No kidding?" The police chief's dull eyes brightened. "What kind of car was it?"

Eleanor looked indignantly at her brother, but Eddy was crafty. "Jaguar XJS. Really shiny new Jaguar."

"It really took off," said Robert solemnly, putting his face in the window of the cruiser. "You know, like greased lightning. You'll never catch him, not a high-class sports car like that. I bet this heap can't do more than seventy."

"Oh, you think so, do you?" The chief's face changed. His bristly jaw clamped shut. His eyes became narrow slits. He gripped the steering wheel, flicked on his siren, jammed his foot on the accelerator, and rammed the cruiser out onto the highway. The big car wallowed left and right, careened and zoomed away, pursuing the speeding madman in the Jaguar XJS.

It found him, sooner than expected. As the seven members of the Children's Crusade rounded a sharp curve half a mile up the road, they came upon the wreckage of the rear-end collision. The chief's big car had rammed into the shining trunk of the Jaguar. The hood of the cruiser was crumpled. The flags flapped at crazy angles. The back of the Jaguar was pleated like an accordion. The two drivers were unhurt. They were standing beside Route 1, shouting at each other and shaking their fists. Another car was pulled up beside them, a cruiser from the police department in North Kingstown, and two huge troopers were grimly writing everything down.

Nobody paid any attention to the ragtag band of children scurrying along beside the highway. But when they were a hundred yards up the road Eddy and Robert looked at each other and whispered a single word, "Totaled," and burst out laughing.

"Totaled?" said Cissie. "What do you mean, totaled?"

"Totally destroyed, smashed, wrecked," chortled Eddy heartlessly. "Both of them, completely pulverized."

"Well, I think that's perfectly terrible," said Frieda in pious horror.

The Cleverness of Carrington

— ☆ —

Inspirited by the day's adventures, they walked too far after supper. When the dusk of evening caught up with them, they were nowhere near a church or a school or a village green. There was nothing to do but stop where they were and try to make themselves comfortable.

They found a likely place, a rocky field on the other side of a strip of dilapidated snow fencing. A lot of big white flowers were scattered in the rough grass. Eleanor had never seen flat white flowers like these. She wondered what they were called. Sleepily the six tired marchers stumbled around the field in the half-light, piling their backpacks against the fence, spreading out their sleeping bags among the flowers.

Only Carrington was wide awake. Carrington had been sleeping soundly on the last leg of the journey. He sat up cheerfully in his stroller, taking a bright interest in what was going on, holding a graham cracker delicately in one hand. He giggled with joy when Cissie handed him his panda. Cissie leaned down and gave him a powerful stare. "*Bingo*, Carrington," she said. "Can you say *Bingo*?"

But Carrington only hugged Bingo and chuckled his deep chuckle.

Frieda was unrolling her sleeping bag beside Carrington's stroller. She didn't say anything, but Cissie knew what she was thinking—*When is that child going to talk? He certainly isn't as smart as me.* It made Cissie mad.

Then in the blaze of headlights Cissie forgot her anger. They all looked up to stare blindly into the glare. At first Georgie thought the dazzling beams were the searchlights of a couple of police cruisers, investigating them, looking them over. But then the whistling and hollering began. It wasn't policemen in police cars. There was too much noise. There were too many crazy lights rushing at them out of the dark.

The big bikes were back. Yelling and screeching, the helmeted riders crashed through the snow fencing and thundered over the uneven ground. Soon they were circling the little camp, uttering bloodcurdling war cries and wild yells like Indians on galloping ponies in the movies. Georgie and Eleanor and Eddy and Robert and Frieda cowered in the middle like pioneers in Conestoga wagons, trying to watch everywhere at once, crowding around Cissie and Carrington, frantic with rage and dismay.

But once again the terrifying menace melted away. Once again the bikes zoomed back to the highway and roared away up the pike. Once again the ordinary buzz and throb of the cars on the road seemed almost like silence. Eleanor and Eddy and Georgie and Frieda and Robert looked at each other and began to breathe again. Their hearts slowed down. Cissie relaxed her hold on Carrington. Carrington calmly began eating his cracker.

Frieda was worried. "I don't like it," she said. "Sooner or later they'll get us. They'll get us for sure."

"Well, they're gone now," said Cissie sensibly. "Let's go to bed."

They were worn out, but they picked up their sleeping bags and moved them close together in a row. Robert collected a pile of cobblestones, just in case. Eleanor made up her mind to stay awake and keep watch. She crawled into her sleeping bag and leaned up on one elbow, listening as Cissie cooed to Carrington and Carrington gurgled softly in reply.

Carrington was whimpering about something. Cissie guessed what he wanted. "No, Carrington, there isn't room for Bingo in this sleeping bag. He's over there on top of the backpacks. See? He's nice and comfortable on the backpacks. You can have him again in the morning."

Carrington stopped whimpering and sucked his thumb.

It was a clear night. Eddy lay on his back and looked up at the sky and pointed out the constellations to Robert—the Northern Cross, the Big Dipper, the North Star.

"If we were going home, we could just follow the North Star," said Robert, sounding a little homesick. "What's that bright star up there?"

"I forget," said Eddy.

"Vega," murmured Eleanor.

"Oh," said Robert.

They stopped talking. After a while Robert muttered, "Locust Underwing."

"What?" said Eddy.

"Moth," said Robert.

"Good night, everybody," whispered Georgie.

Eleanor felt her eyes closing, and she jerked

them open, and made herself stare fixedly at Georgie's flag, which was faintly visible in the dark, moving lightly on its pole. Georgie had stuck the pole in the ground beside a bush. The flag looked very tall. It drooped and lifted and drooped again, then shook itself out and spread itself across the sky.

In the daytime Eleanor's brain was a buzzing mass of twittering agitation, a seething jiggle of plans and counterplans, a dither of swift decisions about what to do in the next five minutes. But now, as her elbow dissolved under her and she fell back, sound asleep, she was soothed by a calming dream.

She wasn't surprised to see the stars in Georgie's flag swarm out of their corner square and dart up and up, and scatter themselves among the constellations, until they were all glowing and pulsing and sparkling in familiar formations against the dark sky. They were Cassiopeia, and Lyra, and Perseus, and the Little Dipper.

That's good, decided Eleanor, smiling to herself with closed eyes. *Georgie's flag isn't just an American flag anymore. It's the flag of the whole world, the whole galaxy. It's the flag of the Milky Way. And that's really nice.*

They were all asleep. All except Carrington.

Carrington's big sister didn't know it, nobody knew it, but Carrington was often awake in the night, lying quietly next to Cissie, his eyes on the sky. Carrington had seen all sorts of things in the sky at night. He had seen red and yellow twinkling lights that made a noise, and little moving lights right over his head, green flashes that sparkled on and off, wandering here and there. He had even seen stars falling out of the sky.

Tonight Carrington lay on his side, staring with longing at the vague shape of Bingo, over there near the fence on top of the backpacks. Therefore he was the only one of the traveling crusaders who knew that a police cruiser was pulling up on the other side of the fence.

Carrington watched as the doors of the cruiser opened. He was surprised when nobody got out of the car. The two big men inside just stayed sitting in the front seat. Carrington could see the red glow of their cigarettes, as they stretched their long legs and leaned back. He didn't understand their words, but he could hear the murmur of their conversation.

". . . lost track of them in Providence," said the police lieutenant at the wheel.

"They've probably given up," said the sergeant. "I bet they're on their way home."

"Maybe they took a bus. You know, with the baby and all, it must have been hard."

"But what if they're camping out someplace? Those ladies in Pawtucket, they said the kids had sleeping bags."

The lieutenant stubbed out his cigarette in the ashtray. "If they didn't go home they'd have to be on this stretch of U.S. One. Come on, let's just keep patrolling this same five or ten miles. We'll find them sooner or later."

The car was going away. It was picking up speed and moving out of sight. Carrington chuckled to himself and wondered what would happen next. He didn't have to wait long. He recognized the drone of the choppers in the distance, and when the noise stopped, he noticed that too. And soon he heard a new sound, although it was hardly a sound at all. It was only a vibration that shook the ground under the sleeping bag. The stars jiggled. Someone was coming with a heavy muffled tread.

Carrington lay keenly awake with his eyes on the road. When the clumsy helmeted silhouettes began moving silently along the fence, he watched them stop and stand in a threatening row, staring down at the sleepers on the ground.

As always, Carrington was interested in everything, excited by the events of each passing day. What was going to happen now? The dark shapes on the other side of the fence were reaching down, picking up the backpacks, slinging them over their shoulders. Then Carrington stiffened and his mouth opened in horrified surprise. One of the helmeted men was snatching up Bingo and stuffing him under one arm as he reached for Robert's backpack. Now he was moving away with the backpack and Carrington's giant panda.

He was taking Bingo! He was taking Bingo away!

And then Carrington, that superbaby who had jiggled and bounced in his stroller over the stony roadsides of Massachusetts and Rhode Island for seventy long miles, Carrington Updike, who had chuckled at every misfortune and laughed at every discomfort, Carrington Chalmers Updike let go at last with a roar of indignation and dismay. "BINGO," bellowed Carrington at the top of his lungs.

There was a moment of rigid shock, and then everything happened at once. The sleepers reared up in their sleeping bags. The thieves cursed and began running heavily down the road with the stolen backpacks.

"After them," cried Frieda, stumbling to her

feet, tripping over her sleeping bag. "Hey, you guys, give those back!"

It was no use. By the time the six crusaders had disentangled themselves from their sleeping bags and stopped running into each other in the dark and found their way at last around one end of the fence, the big bikes were blatting into action a quarter of a mile down the highway. They were backfiring, roaring out onto the road, accelerating, thundering away.

Robert slowed down and stopped running. Eddy spoke strong words of rage and frustration. Eleanor caught Georgie by the hand and gasped for breath. Frieda turned around angrily into another blaze of headlights.

The police lieutenant and the sergeant had found what they were looking for. The sergeant leaned out the car window and shouted at them. "You got a baby? Where's the baby?"

"Here he is," said Cissie, holding up Carrington, who was still sobbing.

"Well, thank the good Lord," said the sergeant. "Now, listen here . . ."

It was too much for Frieda. "You just listen to us," she said, stamping up to the car. "We've just been robbed. It was a whole gang on motorcycles. They stole our backpacks."

Six angry fingers pointed down the road.

"Holy monkey eyes," said the police lieutenant at the wheel.

"Get out of the way, you kids," warned the sergeant, and then the big car plunged onto the highway and took off, its siren wailing.

They watched it go. Eddy shook his head. "They'll never catch up. Those bikes can go a hundred miles an hour, easy. And they've got a head start."

"Hey, looky here," said Robert. "Look what I found." He stooped and picked up something from the ground.

It was Bingo. Carrington made a crooning noise and held out his arms.

"Well, thank goodness," said Cissie. "At least we got something back. What will we do if they don't rescue our knapsacks? All my money was in my knapsack."

Georgie glanced anxiously at Eleanor. She knew what Eleanor was thinking. Without money they would have no choice. They would have to go home.

"Hey, here comes the cruiser again," said Eddy.

Frieda was indignant. She ran to the car as it pulled up beside them with its whining siren and flashing lights. "They got away, didn't they?" she said accusingly. "You let them get away, right?"

"Oh, no," laughed the police lieutenant. "We radioed ahead. There'll be a roadblock a couple miles down U.S. One, just after they come around that big curve there. That'll slow 'em down, you better believe it." He got out of the car and stooped down to look at Georgie. "Are you okay, honey?" He looked at the rest of them. "Are you kids really all right?"

They all nodded their heads vigorously. And then Cissie laughed and held up Carrington in the blue glow of the blinking lights on top of the cruiser. Carrington had stopped crying. He was clutching his enormous panda.

"He said his first word," said Cissie proudly.

"What a smart little boy," cooed Frieda.

Bus Two and the
Green Horror

— ☆ —

When Eleanor woke up, she found herself gazing sleepily at one of the white flowers that grew in the field. The sun was up. And the flower wasn't really a flower at all. It was dirty stuffing, spongy and wet with dew. Eleanor recoiled. Some disgusting piece of mattress or old car seat had been disemboweled in the field, or hurled out of a car to litter the whole side of the road.

Eddy was already up and about, scavenging. "Look," he whispered, bending down to her, holding out a flattened gray rag, "a perfectly good glove. And guess what else I found. Here, hold out your hand."

"Oh, ugh, not another glove," mumbled Eleanor.

"No, no, you'll like it," promised Eddy.

Eleanor pulled her arm out of her sleeping bag into the cold air and held out a gingerly hand. Something small and cool landed in it. It was a strawberry. Eleanor put it in her mouth and closed her eyes, and for an instant the ugliness vanished—the ugliness of the highway, the ugliness of the dirty stuffing, the ugliness of the torn grass where their tormentors had ridden their thundering machines the night before—everything around her disappeared as the strawberry melted on her tongue, tasting as wild and sweet as if it had grown in some fresh meadow at home. Then Eleanor opened her eyes and the ugliness came back. Sighing, she worked her way out of her sleeping bag and stood up.

Soon everybody else was awake. They were up and about, fumbling with their sleeping bags, zipping them up, rolling them into tight bundles.

Cissie woke up Carrington and hauled him off behind a bush. "Not exactly a big tree," she said, grinning, as she brought him back.

They took turns behind the bush, pulling down their trousers, feeling a breeze on their pale bottoms. They picked strawberries. Then they hitched themselves into their knapsacks and began the day's march. Their knapsacks had been returned to them by the police lieutenant the night before. They were as good as ever. Nothing had been stolen. One of Eddy's straps had burst loose, but Eddy fixed it with a safety pin.

Today their destination was Narragansett.

During the morning's march they were back under the watchful eyes of the Rhode Island State Police. Every now and then a cruiser would slow down beside them, and the driver would wave at them, and then the cruiser would speed up again and disappear. When they trudged into Narragansett they found themselves in the welcoming care of the Calvary Bible Church. A committee of women met them at the side of the road and took them straight to the Parish Hall for frankfurters and beans. After supper they slept in the houses of the deacon and the rector and one of the Sunday school teachers. Best of all, they had baths, real baths, with soap and hot water and bubbles and perfumed bath salts. And they washed their filthy clothes in the deacon's and the rector's and the Sunday school teacher's washing machines, and dried them in their dryers. Cissie did two loads, her own and Carrington's. Eddy ruined his best sweater.

"Hey, what's this?" he said, taking a small matted object out of the dryer.

"Oh, no, not your sweater," gasped Eleanor. "You didn't wash your cashmere sweater in the washing machine! You didn't put it in the dryer!"

Eddy giggled, and held the miniature sweater up against himself. "Carrington can have it," he said.

Next morning while they were eating pancakes in the Parish Hall, waited upon by the smiling women of the Calvary Bible Church, they looked up from their plates into a bright flash of light.

"New Haven Register," said the man with the camera. "So, okay, what's this all about?" Then the reporter turned in surprise, as Robert suddenly leaped up from the table and turned his back and hurried away, coughing. "What's the matter with him?"

"I think he got something stuck in his throat," said Eddy.

"Well, listen. I want to know what you kids are up to. It's an anti-Peace Missile march on Washington, is that right? Well, good for you. You're not the only ones scared stiff." He took out his pad and pencil. "Children's Crusade, is that it?"

Eleanor looked down the table and exchanged a glance with Frieda.

"Okay, everybody," whispered Frieda, elbowing Georgie and Cissie, "shut up about those motorcycle guys, okay?"

But there was no need to give an order. They all understood. If their relatives at home found out about the horrible encounter with the motorcycle gang, it would be the end of the march.

And Eleanor didn't want it to be over. Of course she was sick and tired of it, in a way, but she didn't want it to come to an end. She swallowed the last delicious bite of her pancake and looked around the table at her fellow pilgrims. They had started this ridiculous journey, and they might as well finish it.

The days passed, slats of sunshine and bars of darkness. The weather grew warmer. At noon the air shimmered with heat. The faraway approaching cars floated on oily slicks of sky.

When they had been on the road for a week, Cissie's mother suddenly showed up. Once again she tore past them in her Alfa Romeo and jerked to a stop.

"Oh, no," said Cissie. "What now?"

But Mrs. Updike was merely satisfying herself that they were alive and well. She snatched Carrington out of his stroller and held him at arm's length and shook him and hugged him and plopped him down again and barked directions at Cissie and zoomed away in the Alfa Romeo, heading for home.

"Whew," said Cissie.

"Bingo?" said Carrington.

"Here, dear," said Cissie, handing him his panda.

"Okay if I push him now?" said Robert.

Mrs. Updike was like a harbinger, a single ship

heralding the arrival of a fleet. Later that afternoon they were overtaken by a yellow school bus.
Arms waved at them from windows. There were
cheers and screams of greeting.

"Bus Two," cried Georgie. "It's Concord Bus
Two!"

The bus pulled up in front of them and kids
began pouring out, familiar kids, kids they had
grown up with, kids from the Alcott School and
Thoreau and Willard and Peabody and Sanborn.

They had knapsacks on their backs and visored
hats and dangling extra sneakers. They had flashlights and thermoses and three pairs of socks
apiece. They had first-aid kits for emergency use
in the field. They were wild with excitement.

"Permission slips?" cried Frieda, yelling above
the tumult. "You've all got permission slips, I
hope?"

Sidney Bloom's mother waved her pocketbook.
"I've got them right here."

"Frieda's mother put the list in the *Concord
Journal*," said Mrs. Fisher. "So we knew what they
were supposed to bring."

Georgie was ecstatic. Half of the kids in Miss
Brisket's homeroom had come on the bus.

"But why now?" said Eleanor to Mrs. Bloom.
"I mean, what made you decide to come now?"

"*The Boston Globe*. They printed your picture in the *Globe*. I guess it was passed along by the *Providence Journal*. It got the whole town excited. All the kids wanted to come."

"But it's not just that," said Sidney.

"No, that's right," said Mrs. Bloom.

Sidney looked at the other kids who had come on the bus, and they stopped milling around and crowded in close and looked at Sidney soberly.

"The President gave this talk on TV," explained Sidney gravely. "He says they've finished building the Peace Missile. They're shipping it out west to Nevada. They've got this big launching platform out there in Nevada."

"Oh, is that it?" said Eleanor.

Then the mothers made their farewells, embellished with good advice, and climbed back on the bus, and the bus driver waved and wished them good luck, and then he pulled the bus out onto Route 1, heading the other way.

The grown-ups were gone. Once more it was just kids, nothing but kids. The new ones went berserk with the thrill of being on their own. They squealed and shouted and jumped up and down.

Frieda had to yell very loud to call everybody to order: "NOW HEAR THIS." And then she explained the rules. "No pushing or shoving. And, look, you see that white line on the edge of the road? Well, listen, everybody has to stay *strictly* on this side of the white line. And you can't march more than two together. Okay? Have you got that?" She was making up new rules as she went along, responding to this new crisis like a general in the field.

For Eleanor, life suddenly looked more difficult. Instead of a friendly bunch of sturdy old friends and companions—four girls, two boys and a baby—there would now be sixty-four people in the Children's Crusade. How would they know if anybody was lost? She would have to count noses all the time.

And most of the new kids looked young, terribly young. Eleanor would have been grateful for a new flock of eighth graders, but these kids weren't even from junior high. Some kind of fever seemed to have swept the fourth and fifth grades.

"How old are *you?*" said Eleanor accusingly, looking down at Otis Fisher. Otis was only about three and a half feet tall.

"I'm nine years old," answered Otis smartly. "Ask Georgie. I'm in her homeroom. My whole family is of small stature. My father's a Phi Beta Kappa. He has a Ph.D."

"Well, no *kidding*. I'm really *impressed*."

Then somebody told on Weezie Hoskins. Weezie, it turned out, was only in second grade. "I've got a permission slip," said Weezie pugnaciously, as Eleanor stared at her in horror.

Eleanor groaned. If ever there was a hopeless-looking specimen for a walking journey of hundreds of miles, it was Weezie Hoskins. Weezie was a frail-looking scrawny girl with a harum-scarum look and a glittering little shifty eye.

"My mother said it was okay," insisted Weezie.

There were ripples of amusement among the other kids from the bus. Sidney Bloom took Eleanor aside. "Her mother's—you know—" Sidney made a circle beside his head. "Weezie's better off with us. Honest."

Then Weezie spoke up sharply for herself. "What about Cissie's little brother? He can't even walk, for shit's sake."

Frieda was scandalized. Instantly she made another rule. "No swearing on this march! Does everybody hear that? NO SWEARING ON THIS PILGRIMAGE."

Eleanor huddled with Eddy and Frieda. "Look at her," complained Eleanor. "She's so small. She'll never make it."

"What can we do?" said Eddy. "The bus has gone home."

"We can call her mother at the next gas station," said Frieda angrily. "And tell her she has to come and get her daughter."

But it was too much to decide. They let it pass. Weezie saw craftily that they had given up, and she crowded into the front of the procession, pretending she didn't see Frieda's scowl.

It was time to get started. "OKAY," yelled Frieda, holding her hands beside her mouth, "LET'S GO." Then she turned in surprise. "Oh, Robert, there you are. Hey, where have you been?"

Robert shrugged his shoulders, and got in line beside Eddy.

And then they were off, the new marchers striding along with the old. They were eager and willing, they were ready to march to Washington, to Texas, to Brazil. Sidney Bloom had brought along his recorder. It sounded like a penny whistle. Soon he had everybody singing "I Been Working on the Railroad," and "Row, Row, Row Your Boat." Then he taught them "We Shall Overcome."

We shall over-co-o-ome,

sang Sidney,

We shall over-co-o-ome,
We shall overcome! some! day-ay-ay-ay-ay!

Oh-oh, deep in my heart,
I do believe,
We shall overcome—some—day!

It was a thrilling song. Eleanor was surprised to feel tears in her eyes. She walked along behind Sidney and Frieda, singing the second verse,

We are not afrai-ai-aid,

trying as usual to avoid the litter beside the road, stumbling over a wad of plastic, disentangling herself from a flying grocery bag. Georgie pulled Eleanor's arm and looked up at her with glowing eyes. For a moment, just while they were singing, the whole march seemed embodied in the song. Georgie's flag tumbled and pulsed and rippled as though it were dancing in time to the music.

But, as always, the road went on unwinding in front of them. The singing trailed off and stopped. Eleanor could guess what the new marchers were thinking. They were beginning to realize that walking to Washington really and truly meant *walking* to Washington. The cars rushed past them unceasingly. A succession of oil trucks overtook them, and for a few minutes the roar of their huge engines and the screaming whine of their enormous tires pounded in everybody's head and filled all the world. *You see?* said Eleanor silently to the people who were marching along Route 1 for the first time. *This is what it's like.*

And then they had yet another volunteer. Eleanor was walking at the very end of the procession to make sure they weren't losing any stragglers, when a car with a shuddering engine drew up beside her. Its muffler was gone. It made a terrible noise.

Firmly Eleanor kept her face forward, ignoring the throbbing menace at her side, waiting for it to satisfy its curiosity and pick up speed and zoom away. But instead there was a shriek of clashing gears, and then the car continued to chug along at five miles an hour. A sensation of greenness filled the left side of Eleanor's vision. She began to get a queer feeling. The noise and the clashing gears and the greenness were familiar. She glanced sideways at the car, then laughed in helpless vexation. It was Oliver's car. It was Oliver Winslow in the Green Horror, Oliver Winslow in his hideous Chevy Impala.

But Eddy was delighted. "Oliver, you fixed it," he shouted, and he ran back to slap the rattling hood and put his head in the open window. "Did that police chief put you in jail?"

"Oh, no, he was too busy trying to get his own

car fixed. The town council, they didn't want to pay for a new front end. He didn't have time for me." Oliver grinned at the kids who were swarming around his car, throwing open the doors, jumping in and bouncing on the Chevy's dusty plush seats.

"Hey, you kids, get off the road," screamed Eleanor.

"NOW HEAR THIS," shrieked Frieda, making up a new rule. "Anybody who goes over the white line has to go home."

Georgie knew the rules too. She looked at Eleanor earnestly. "He can't stay, can he? We can't have anybody in a car. I mean, we have to walk. Everybody has to walk."

Eleanor nodded and patted Georgie's shoulder, and then she stuck her head in the car on the driver's side and spoke sternly to Oliver. "Listen, Oliver, I *told* you not to come. You're too old. I told you, right? And no cars. Remember what I said? No cars."

"Well, I just thought—" Oliver grinned at her and shrugged. Then he wiped his big red face and laughed awkwardly. His earring shook. He was wearing his greasy Australian hat, one side fastened jauntily to the crown with a safety pin.

Eddy leaned over the front seat from the back,

where he was crowded in with three or four smaller kids. "Listen," he said to Eleanor, "why don't we just have one car, okay? I mean somebody might get sick, and then they could ride in the car until we get to the next town. What will we do if one of the kids gets sick?"

Eleanor started to protest, and then she thought better of it. She pulled her head out of the car and looked at Weezie Hoskins, who was bouncing on the front bumper. Weezie was so small and skinny, it didn't seem possible she could ever walk three hundred and fifty miles. She looked like some kind of brittle little insect. Well, of course Georgie looked frail too, but Eleanor knew Georgie was really terrifically strong. Her flimsy little body was propelled forward by her tremendously powerful will. But Weezie didn't look like a person with any willpower. Look at her! She was jumping off the bumper, landing on Otis Fisher. Otis yelled and swatted her. Weezie swatted back. A troublemaker, that was what she was going to be, thought Eleanor grimly. And feeble at the same time. Before they got all the way to Washington, D.C., Weezie Hoskins might be needing the help of Oliver Winslow and the Green Horror.

So Oliver stayed. Frieda invented another rule.

Oliver was to stay strictly in the rear, a hundred yards back, so that he wouldn't drive over the last ragtag kids by mistake. But from now on the Green Horror would travel with them. It was an official part of the march to Washington, the Children's Crusade, the Pilgrimage of Peace.

A Proliferation of Flags

— ☆ —

At the White House, interest in the Children's Crusade was working its way up. *The Boston Globe* story had traveled from the Office of Grass Roots Information to the White House Office of Public Relations to the Office of the Deputy Press Secretary. The Deputy Press Secretary took it to the Hay-Adams Hotel, where he was having lunch with the President's Personal Advisor, Charley Chase.

He passed the clipping across the table while Charley ate his grapefruit.

Charley glanced at the picture and ran his eye down the article. Then he wiped his mouth on his napkin and laughed. "Look," he said, "they'll never make it. It would take a month. They're just little kids. Wait till they get caught in a good rainstorm. That will be the end of the whole thing."

— ☆ —

David Klein stood beside the President's desk and read his winning letter in a firm voice. "To me the flag of my country stands for my own city of New York, and for the Central European immigrants who came here to settle in the new land. It stands for the Jews who found safety in our busy streets, and education for their children, and work to do, hard work. It stands for the tall buildings that rise between the East River and the Hudson. . . ."

"Excellent," said the President, as David paused and lowered his sheet of paper and looked at him nervously. "That's a fine job, young man. I appreciate it."

David cleared his throat. "But Mr. President, that's not all. As a matter of fact, there's another paragraph . . ."

The President jumped to his feet. "Now, boy, that's quite enough. Come on, you've got work to do. There's a delegation of registered nurses waiting for us in the Rose Garden." He strode out the door of the Oval Office, and David had no choice but to follow him, carrying the sparkling flag.

It was no longer the only flag of its kind. The new presidential flag was everywhere. There were cheap imitations for sale on the street corners of all the big cities in the country, in Los Angeles, in Milwaukee, in Memphis and Tallahassee. In Nashua, New Hampshire, the Grand Master of the Grange bought a bunch of them to decorate the Grange Hall. In Chicago the Rotary Club ordered a thousand to display in the stores whose owners belonged to the Club. And in Concord, Massachusetts, a bucket of the new flags stood on the sidewalk outside the ten-cent store on Walden Street.

Uncle Freddy saw them there as he went into the dime store to buy a pair of socks. He stopped and stared. The little flags were shoddily made. The God-Bless-America message was merely stamped across the stripes in mustard-colored ink. The cheap glitter on the stars was shedding all over the sidewalk.

They were imposters, decided Uncle Freddy angrily, just like the original flag itself, the one in the President's office. The presidential flag was not really the flag of the United States at all. It had taken over the White House, but could it take over the whole country? It stood for the Peace Missile. It stood for billions of dollars in nuclear weapons. It stood for destruction.

But Georgie's flag was marching to meet it, to oppose it, stripe for stripe, and star for star. Where were they now, those children, moving at their snail-like pace across the map of New England? Last night Eleanor had called home from Perryville, Rhode Island. They were still far away from their destination, so far away from Washington, D.C.!

Uncle Freddy bought his socks and walked back down Walden Street, thinking about the two flags coming closer and closer to each other. Would the two flags ever meet? Would Georgie and the President ever come face to face?

Oh, Fame! Oh, Glory!

— ☆ —

The new marchers from Concord were more privileged than the old. It would be a long time before they had to sleep beside the highway. Every day the Children's Crusade was passed along from one bunch of hospitable grown-ups to another.

In Charlestown it was the Policemen's Benefit Association. In Westerly it was the Altar Guild of the Episcopal Church. In Groton, Connecticut, it was the school committee and the principal of Fitch Junior High School.

But before they reached Westerly and Groton, they ran into a television cameraman. He was waiting for them in Haversham, Rhode Island. He had driven his Channel 10 van all the way down from Providence.

Providence! Eleanor tried to remember Providence, but it was too far back. They had been lost in Providence. It had been like a bad dream, going around and around, she remembered that, but it all seemed a long time ago.

"How long did it take you?" she asked curiously. "I mean, to get here from Providence?"

"An hour," said the man carelessly, glancing at his watch. "Listen, I got a coupla other things to do, so tell me what you're try'n'a do. *The Boston Globe*, it had a story."

Frieda explained. Sidney jumped in, too, talking fast, his skinny arms waving. All the new marchers were thrilled. They crowded around the cameraman.

Eleanor stood in the background with Georgie, feeling a little sour. The new kids had hardly even got their shoes dirty, and here they were, all talking at once, being glamorous on TV.

"Okay, okay," shouted the cameraman. "Now get in line, okay? Like you're walking? Who's the little kid with the flag? Get her up front. No, wait, the baby, put the baby in front, okay? Now walk, okay? Just walk. Right. Now, why don'tcha smile, okay, everybody? Okay, okay, that's it."

Swiftly the cameraman from Providence packed up his equipment, stuffed it in his van, and sped away.

"Hey," said Weezie Hoskins, running up to Georgie and Eleanor. "Guess what? I thumbed my nose at the camera. Honest, I really did." Weezie thumbed her nose at Eleanor and tittered.

Eleanor groaned and closed her eyes. It was hopeless. The whole thing was absolutely hopeless.

Frieda ran up and down the line, counting noses. "Sixty-two, sixty-three. Hey, only sixty-three? Somebody's missing! Who's missing?"

But then Eddy laughed and pointed at the McDonald's sign up ahead, OVER 45 BILLION SERVED. Robert was coming out from behind the sign with his butterfly net, sauntering back to them, looking around vaguely as though there were nothing on his mind but Swallowtails and Admirals and Painted Ladies.

"NOW HEAR THIS," shouted Frieda, glaring at Robert. "From now on, everybody has to march with the same partner, okay? So we'll know right away if anybody's missing. And nobody goes ANYWHERE without telling me first, right?"

Poor Frieda! Her task was impossible. The sixty-three other members of the Children's Crusade refused to march in orderly pairs. Instead they were a milling, jiggling mass of slight bodies moving more or less in the same direction. If they had been adults they would have marched forward at the same rate with a steady rhythmical motion. But they were kids, and therefore they were a random tide that washed this way and that, with wild hopping here and there, and darting and teasing. The whole procession heaved and tumbled. It was a miracle that no one was side-swiped by a speeding car. Frieda did a lot of miscellaneous screaming. To Eleanor it had begun to seem impossible that they would ever get anywhere.

And yet they did.

Next day they were in Mystic, Connecticut. It was the best place they had found so far. Mystic was on the Atlantic Ocean. There were little coves and inlets, with sailboats tilting sideways on the water, their sails bellying out in sun and shadow. There was a big bridge to cross. They had to wait while it lifted up to allow a tall-masted boat to run out to sea. Beyond the bridge at the top of the hill there was a white church so beautiful that Georgie wondered if it was full of angels.

And it was, as it turned out—angels in the form of the Hospitality Committee and the Women's Fellowship of the Baptist Union Church. They were standing behind tables loaded with lunch, beaming at the crusaders, offering them sandwiches and lemonade and chocolate cake.

Georgie and Eleanor and Frieda and Robert and Eddy and Sidney and everybody else swarmed around the tables and ate everything, down to the last crumb. Oliver Winslow ate half a cake. And then they thanked the Hospitality Committee and the Women's Fellowship and walked down, down, down the hill on the other side, to fields full of cows and more views of the sea. They sang as they walked, "On Top of Old Smoky" and "I Been Working on the Railroad."

But by midafternoon they were back in strip country. The huge signs rose ahead of them—

LONG HILL LIQUORS

T.J. MAX

BURGER KING

RADIO SHACK

POQUONICK CHIROPRACTIC

After the refreshing loveliness of the little town of Mystic, it seemed unbearable. The day turned hot. They stopped singing and straggled along the road. Carrington's stroller bounced. Eddy taught his car game to a bunch of fifth graders, and soon they were all in hot dispute about the number of points a BMW was worth, or a Nissan sports coupe. Georgie marched in the front line, then ran back, her flag bobbing over her shoulder, to find Frieda. Frieda was glad to see her. Frieda had given up being a decision maker and lawgiver. She was taking a turn as rear guard.

And then they saw the vans. It was not just one TV van this time. It was three of them and a pickup truck.

At first Eleanor thought the black objects mounted on the pickup were machine guns. But then as the pickup began moving toward them, she could see that they were cameras. The truck drove past them smoothly, cameras rolling. Eleanor didn't know which way to look. She stared forward and marched straight ahead, wondering if Weezie Hoskins was thumbing her nose.

Then Eleanor caught her breath. Her heart quickened. A smart-looking man in a fancy raincoat was getting out of one of the vans. He was famous. He was Derek Cherniak, the TV anchorman. He was looking at Eleanor. He was walking right up to her with a microphone, a cameraman at his side.

Eleanor's step faltered. She slowed down and stopped. The entire procession stopped, too, and stared, enraptured, at Derek Cherniak. Eleanor wished she could comb her hair, or pull a Kleenex out of her pocket and lick it and wipe her face. But she was too dignified to do that. She could feel her dignity rivet her features in a blank stare and lock her bones together.

From close up, Derek Cherniak was even more handsome than on TV. He had a kind of glossy shine. He spoke politely to Eleanor, and his words were as calm and serene as they were every morning on the news. "Can you tell me where you kids are going, and why you're going there?"

For Eleanor it was a moment of crisis, an instant of temptation. Why shouldn't she talk to Derek Cherniak and appear in all the living rooms of the nation? For a second she imagined her French teacher, Mr. Orth, at home in Concord, admiring a lovely TV image of Eleanor Hall talking on the network news about the Children's Crusade. Oh, fame! Oh, glory! And then Eleanor tossed it all aside. She was too old. It was Georgie's crusade, not Eleanor's. The march belonged to the younger kids, not to somebody who was practically grown up. "It was Georgie's idea," she said. "You should talk to Georgie. She's my little sister. Well, really, she's my stepcousin." Confused, Eleanor turned around, looking for Georgie. But Georgie was far away. Her flag was sticking up at the end of the line.

Then Frieda galloped up to save the day. "I'm the Media Interface Person," she said firmly. "You can talk to me."

Aunt Alex and Uncle Freddy saw them on the morning news. Laughing, pointing at the screen, they picked out Eleanor and Eddy and Frieda, and Cissie and Carrington. They caught a quick glimpse of Georgie as the camera panned along the line, but there was no sign of Robert Toby.

It was a relief to see them, Eleanor and Eddy and Georgie, to look at their sunburned faces, to know they were really all right. "They look well, don't you think?" said Uncle Freddy anxiously.

Aunt Alex laughed. "Did you see how dirty Eddy is?" Then she stopped laughing. "What on earth will happen when they actually arrive in Washington? I mean, I can't picture it. I just can't see Georgie talking to the President, reading him her letter, can you? He'll just mow her down with logic. He'll explain everything to her reasonably. He'll go from A to B to C to D. You know, all that rational Pentagon argument about increasing our nuclear deterrent and keeping up with the Russians. Poor Georgie! She'll just stand there. What can she say? She's only a little girl."

"Ah, but that's just the point. She hasn't been corrupted with small print about the balance of tactical and strategic weapons. She hasn't been sitting in an office in artificial light. She's got her head up in the sunshine where she can see the obvious truth that they are blind to."

"Oh, I know. You mean, *A little child shall lead them*." Aunt Alex was quoting from the Bible. She sighed. "That's an awfully big responsibility for one poor skinny little fourth-grade girl."

"Actually," said Uncle Freddy, "I was thinking about the Emperor's New Clothes." His face took on a foolish look of childlike innocence as he gazed upward at the ceiling. " 'Oh, sir,' Georgie will say, like the little boy in the story, 'have you noticed you're about to blow up the world?' And then the President will stagger back in surprise, and say, 'I am? Why, good heavens, so I am.' "

There was a loud knock at the front door. It was their nosy neighbor, Madeline Prawn. She was standing on the front porch, holding a notebook. On the front of her blouse she wore a pin in the shape of the Presidential flag, with *God Bless America* written across the enameled stripes in 24-karat gold.

"I wonder if you could tell me," said Miss Prawn, "how your children got the idea of marching to Washington." She looked at them archly. "You people put them up to it, didn't you? Come on now, confess!"

"No, no," said Aunt Alex hastily. "It was their own idea entirely."

"But aren't you worried? All those little children on the highway? The danger from all those high-speed cars? I should think you would be seriously concerned about their health and safety."

Uncle Freddy looked at Aunt Alex. "No, no," he said bravely, his face pale and drawn, "not at all."

Aunt Alex, too, was shaking her head violently. "No, not a bit, not at all. No, no, no, not at all."

Veronica Joins Up

— ☆ —

The Children's Crusade was famous. Everyone had seen them on television with Derek Cherniak. From now on, nothing was the same.

In Old Lyme, Connecticut, a couple of sixth graders tried to join them, but they didn't have permission slips, so Frieda sent them home.

In Old Saybrook they were met by the mayor, who gave Sidney the key to the city. Sidney said thank you, and took the key carefully in both hands. It weighed a ton. He handed it back apologetically. "Would it be okay to send it to the Sanborn School on Old Marlboro Road in Concord, Massachusetts? I mean, it's pretty heavy to carry, and we've got a long way to go."

"Zip code zero one seven four two," said Frieda helpfully.

And on the way to Madison, they had another

encounter with national television. This time the television van was accompanied by a silver car.

Eddy whistled. "Porsche Carrera coupe," he said. The van and the car pulled up and stopped, dead ahead. A couple of people got out of the van and bustled around, mounting a camera on a rolling cart and trundling it back until it was parallel with the first pair of marchers. But they didn't aim the camera at Eleanor and Frieda, they pointed it back at the silver car.

"Just keep going," muttered Frieda. "That car is going to have to get out of the way. Who do they think they are?"

Then they all stared, as a small figure emerged from the silver car and began walking toward them.

The camera rolled.

Eleanor narrowed her eyes. The girl was coming closer and closer. She was smiling. She was beautiful. She looked familiar in the same way Derek Cherniak had looked familiar, because she was famous.

Eleanor caught her breath. "Veronica Glassmore," she hissed between her teeth. "What's *she* doing here?"

Veronica was slowing down. She paused in front of the camera. "I have come to join your great pilgrimage," she said loudly. "I want to march with you, side by side."

"Well, all right, go ahead," said Eleanor sharply. "Why not?" But she didn't stop walking when she came to Veronica. She marched right past her, along with Frieda and Eddy and Georgie and the flag.

Instantly Veronica was engulfed by marching children. She was facing the wrong way. Astonished, she turned around and shouldered her way back to the front. Soon she was prancing along with Eleanor and Frieda, beaming triumphantly at the camera, which was retreating smoothly in front of them, recording the thrilling moment of Veronica Glassmore's enlistment in the Children's Crusade.

Eleanor was indignant. She dropped back to walk with Cissie. Frieda and Eddy melted away. Georgie was nowhere to be seen. Veronica was left at the head of the procession all by herself.

"Actually," murmured Frieda, squeezing in beside Eleanor and Cissie, "I suppose we should be glad. You know, because she's important. When Veronica Glassmore does something, people pay attention. She could make people sit up and take notice of the whole pilgrimage."

"Well, good for her," said Eleanor sarcastically.

The TV van was leaving. The silver car remained, moving along sleekly at the front of the procession. Eddy snickered. "Kind of different from Oliver's car, right? The silver Porsche, *ta-dah!* and the Green Horror, *rattle-rattle-clank!*"

Cissie Updike felt sorry for Veronica. She pushed Carrington's stroller to the front and walked beside her. "Listen," she said kindly, "maybe you ought to tell your driver he can leave now. We're not supposed to have any cars on this crusade. No grown-ups. That's the rule."

Veronica looked at her in surprise. "But my agent's in the car. She's got all my stuff."

"Why don't you carry a backpack like the rest of us?"

"Oh, I couldn't possibly carry everything in a backpack," protested Veronica.

"Well, listen," said Cissie earnestly, "it's just that your car really shouldn't be here. It doesn't belong in the crusade."

Veronica looked cross. She stared down at Carrington and said meanly, "Isn't that baby awfully dirty?"

"Bingo!" said Carrington, with an angelic smile.

That evening the pilgrimage was welcomed by another congregation, the people of Temple Beth Tikvah in Madison. They had prepared a huge

supper in the social hall of the temple, and hung
a big banner across the wall,

CHILDREN'S CRUSADE,
SHALOM!!!

"What's 'Shalom'?" said Eddy to Robert.
"Peace, I think," said Robert.
Their paper plates were soon heaped with food.
The Rabbi made a speech. He called them heroes,
and everybody cheered. The heroes basked in the
Rabbi's praise, and asked for second helpings.
"Oh, thank you," said Cissie gratefully. "It's just
delicious. More macaroni, Carrington?"

After supper Veronica was busy. She an-
nounced graciously that she would sign auto-
graphs, and then for a while she scribbled her
name on scraps of paper, the backs of envelopes,
and paper napkins. After that she flitted around
the big room, introducing herself to her fellow
crusaders.

Eleanor watched her talk to Sidney. Sidney was
pointing at Georgie, gesturing, waving his arms,
pointing at Georgie again. Then Veronica moved
in on Frieda. Frieda listened and stared at the
wall and pushed her big glasses up on her nose,
and then she, too, wagged her head in Georgie's

direction. After Frieda, Veronica buttonholed somebody else.

"What was that all about?" said Eleanor to Frieda.

"Oh, she really seems interested in everybody," said Frieda. "She was asking a lot of questions. You know, about how the whole thing got started."

"Did you tell her about Georgie?"

"Well, of course. Naturally. I mean, it's Georgie's march. Everybody knows that."

"Oh, sure," said Eleanor, but she watched uneasily as Veronica cornered Georgie and sat down beside her on a folding chair. Georgie sat shyly, her chin buried in the neck of her turtleneck shirt, her hands between her knees, while Veronica gazed at her and talked a blue streak.

Veronica was doing something important. She was conducting an undercover investigation. She was the personal secret agent of the assistant to the President, Charley Chase. Now she stared at Georgie, convinced that she had come to the heart of her secret inquiry. Georgie didn't look like a Big Wheel to Veronica, but all the others said she was right in the middle of everything. So Veronica moved her chair closer, nudging the staff of Georgie's flag, which was leaning against Georgie's chair. The flag flowed down over their shoulders and knees, quivering restlessly in the little breezes that were set in motion by the busy comings and goings in the social hall of Temple Beth Tikvah.

Then Veronica stopped talking. For a moment she swayed in her chair. She was feeling dizzy. Something very strange was happening. The basement hall and all the people of Temple Beth Tikvah were drifting away. She was floating out of her chair, surrounded by an immensity of empty space. Below her the sun turned on its axis, fiery and far away, and around it the planets were bathed in light. She could see the spinning earth, blue and beautiful, and the moon moving around it like a ball on a string.

And then Veronica's heart stopped, and she cried, "No, no!"

Something terrible was happening to the familiar planet that was the earth. It was flaring up and burning brightly. And then as she watched in horror, the fire went out and the earth went on spinning and moving slowly in its ancient orbit around the sun, but now it was a blackened cinder, like a piece of coal.

Veronica gripped the edge of her chair, her heart thumping. She closed her eyes and opened them again. To her intense relief she found herself back in the social hall of Temple Beth Tikvah with the sixty-four members of the Children's

Crusade and the entire congregation of the Temple. The grown-ups were gathering up the paper plates and plastic forks and clashing the pots in the kitchen. The pilgrims of the Children's Crusade were helping with the cleanup, running around with wastebaskets. Furtively Veronica glanced at Georgie. Had Georgie seen it too? The destruction of the earth? Her face was ashy white. She was staring at the air in front of her with hollow eyes. The flag hung slack.

And then Veronica hardened her heart. She put aside the vision she had seen, and remembered only why she had seen it. She had discovered the secret of the Children's Crusade. It was Georgie, Georgie and the flag. They were the secret. The flag and the girl who carried it.

Across the room, Eleanor watched as Veronica stood up, wobbling a little on her feet, then making a beeline for Robert Toby. Eleanor laughed as Robert jumped out of his chair and blundered away, tripping over folding chairs.

Eleanor sat down beside Georgie. "What did she say, Georgie, dear?"

"Oh, she wanted to know why I decided to go to Washington," murmured Georgie, her lips pale, her eyes on her knees. "And all about the flag and everything."

"Did you tell her?"

Georgie shook her head. "I was too scared."

Next morning it was raining.

The rabbi and all the volunteer cooks urged the crusaders to stay and wait for better weather. But they were eager to be on their way. They thanked the rabbi and the cooks for the delicious supper and the wonderful breakfast and the comfortable cushions on the floor of the social hall, and then they put on their parkas and ponchos and raincoats and set off in the rain.

But it was no fun. Their good spirits vanished. All the excitement of marching and singing together disappeared in the downpour, and the thrill of having a grand destination and a noble cause. They sloshed along Route 1, splashed by passing cars, tramping around puddles. Weezie Hoskins clung to Eleanor's raincoat, whining. Everyone's sneakers were soaked. Carringon's thick winter snowsuit was spattered with mud.

Veronica Glassmore spent the soggy morning in her silver car. But when the television van came back at noon, she was ready. The TV team found her swinging along the side of the road at the front of the procession, wearing a transparent raincoat and carrying a transparent umbrella. Her hair was dry and shining, curled and puffed in the car with a hotcomb plugged into the cigarette lighter.

"Veronica," said Frannie Mears, the celebrity interviewer, "what do you think of the ideals and goals of the Children's Crusade?"

"Well, I just think it's so important," said Veronica in high seriousness. "I mean peace is so important in the world. I mean, to every man, woman, and child."

"And a little bit of rain doesn't bother you?"

"Oh, no," laughed Veronica. "Who cares about a little rain when something so, you know, important, is going on?"

The camera backed away and took more footage of the Children's Crusade—first Veronica in the lead, and then Cissie Updike and her baby brother, and then the solid mass of serious marchers, their heads down, their backs bowed to the rain, their faces glum.

Once again the TV van drove away. Veronica scurried back to her car, folded up her umbrella, and jumped in. Grouchy catcalls and rude remarks floated up from the procession. But before long, Veronica emerged again, and splashed back to Eleanor.

"Listen," she said, "have you heard about the Flag Brigade? I just heard this item on the radio."

"No," muttered Eleanor. "The Flag Brigade? What's that?"

"It's kids like you. Only on the other side. A whole lot of kids. They've organized a crusade to support the President. You know, hordes of them. They've all got these beautiful sparkly flags, and they're marching around Washington, D.C. They've got cheerleaders and a whole lot of really good cheers."

Eleanor said nothing. Her heart sank.

"And uniforms. Bright blue. You know, it's not just kids for peace anymore, or anything like that. It's kids against kids."

Eleanor wanted to cry. She could feel her throat fill up. For the first time since she had left home, she wanted to sit down and sob. It was too much. She couldn't bear it. The whole point of their crusade was lost. The whole point was kids, kids marching against the Peace Missile. If there were other kids marching on the other side, it just canceled their side out. It just made them look foolish. *Kids against kids.* Eleanor felt betrayed. She stared straight ahead and hoped the wetness in her eyes would look like rain.

"I just thought you ought to know," said Veronica, and then she flounced back to her car and climbed in.

For ten minutes the car continued to purr at

the head of the procession, its whitewall tires sending up a tiny spray, and then it suddenly gathered speed and zoomed away, throwing a splashing shower over Sidney and Eddy, who were taking their turn being first in line.

The President Feels
a Draft

—☆—

The news about the Children's Crusade had reached the Oval Office at last. Charley Chase replayed Frieda's television interview with Derek Cherniak for President Toby.

The President was fascinated. He sat forward and stared as the procession filed across the screen, the long trailing line of children marching two by two, the last child carrying a big flag.

And then Veronica Glassmore appeared with the Children's Crusade, walking gallantly in the rain, flashing her dazzling smile.

Charley laughed, and turned down the volume control. "You wouldn't think so after that episode, but Veronica Glassmore is on our side."

The President was amused. "On our side? You mean she's a spy? She came forward and volunteered?"

"Well, she didn't exactly volunteer." Charley made a face. "We got hold of her agent and haggled over a price, and then she agreed to help us out. She's trying to find out what these kids intend to do. And we had a little suggestion of our own. She's spreading discouraging rumors down the line. Our hope is they'll give up before long and go home. Look at them, poor little rats, splashing along in the rain. They won't be able to take much more of that." Charley grinned, and gestured at the windows. The wind was hurling raindrops relentlessly against the glass. "I understand it's going to go on like that all week." Then Charley glanced at the clock on the President's desk. "Holy cow, look at the time. I'd better run over to the south door and meet the Secretary of State and General Sedgewick."

Mrs. Colefax put her head in the door as Charley hurried out. "The new flag bearer is here, Mr. President."

"Well, show her in," said President Toby. He turned to smile at the eighth-grade girl as she came shyly into the Oval Office. Raindrops were sparkling on her dark braids and dripping from her raincoat on the yellow carpet.

"Maria Verdade, from New Mexico," said Mrs. Colefax. "Here, dear, I'll take your coat."

There was just time for Maria to read her letter

to the President before the meeting with the Secretary of State and General Sedgewick. She stood erect in front of the brass fire screen and read the letter aloud, while the President listened respectfully. Maria's letter described the villages of the Navaho Indians, and the old Spanish missions, and the Santa Fe trail. It turned poetic as Maria painted a picture of the colors of the desert in the spring of the year, and the rainbow-wide skies of New Mexico. To Maria Verdade the stars and stripes meant the Land of Sunshine, her own home state.

The President applauded enthusiastically.

"Oh, but I'm not finished yet," said Maria, screwing up her courage. "I just wanted to say—"

"Never mind," said the President quickly. "I'm sorry, my dear, but I have an important meeting right now. I hope you'll join me at six o'clock for the state dinner with the President of Portugal. Mrs. Colefax will tell you what to do."

Maria said good-bye, a little crestfallen, and the President went to the window to look out at the rain-swept driveway. Limousines were pulling up to the awning that led to the Diplomatic Reception Room where Charley would be waiting for the new arrivals.

It was indeed going to be an important meeting. There was trouble abroad. All over Europe protest was mounting against the Peace Missile. Anti-nuclear groups in Holland and West Germany were making a hullabaloo. The British Parliament was in an uproar. The Canadian Prime Minister and the President of Mexico were calling for a North American summit conference. And of course right here in Washington there was turmoil on Capitol Hill. Congress was at the President's throat. Something had to be done. This morning, with the help of the Secretary of State and General Sedgewick, the President hoped to compose some kind of statement to calm things down.

But then as Mrs. Colefax opened the door to usher in General Sedgewick, the President remembered the children on the road, far to the northeast. Suddenly, uncontrollably, a tremor shook him.

"Are you all right, sir?" said General Sedgewick, slapping his wet hat with its four gold stars against his knee. "Not coming down with something, I hope?"

"Oh, no, it's just this rain. I felt a draft from the door," said the President.

The Rebirth of the Crusade

— ☆ —

It rained for three days.

At the end of the third day, drenched and discouraged, the children of the Crusade spent the night in the gymnasium of the Fair Haven Middle School in New Haven, Connecticut, as guests of the Parent-Teacher Association. They festooned their sopping clothes all over the gym. Blue jeans were draped over parallel bars, socks were suspended from climbing ladders, sweaters were knotted between shinny ropes and knee rings. The shoestrings of sneakers were tied together and hung from every available hook. Eddy tossed a couple of T-shirts high in the air, and kept tossing them until they landed on the hoops of the basketball nets.

But in the morning everything was still soggy. The sun came up, menacing and huge, ragged at the edges and out of shape. The day promised to be moist and sweltering.

There was nothing they could do about it. Wet or dry, clothing had to be stuffed into mildewed knapsacks. Feet had to be squeezed into squelching sneakers. Gloomily the sodden pilgrims ate breakfast in the school cafeteria and thanked the PTA and set out for Bridgeport. At the end of the first mile they were already tired. They stumbled along in the humid heat, complaining. Some of the younger children were sniffling.

They would never make it to Bridgeport, not that day. Their progress was too slow. It was too hot. The black asphalt of the highway absorbed the heat of the sun and gave it back like a frying pan.

And stupid things kept happening. During the second hour there was a screech at the end of the line. Eleanor ran back to find Angela Wanzer sitting on the gritty road, weeping bitterly, nursing a pair of skinned knees.

"I didn't do it," said Weezie Hoskins slyly, grinning at Eleanor.

But the others accused her angrily. "She did too! She pushed her from behind!"

It was a genuine emergency in the field, decided Eleanor. Putting down her backpack, she poked among her soggy possessions for her first-aid kit. Soon Angela was patched up with disinfectant and big squares of gauze and strips of adhesive tape. She limped along, holding Eleanor's hand, tears trickling down her cheeks.

Weezie was unrepentant. An hour later she pinched Debbie Farnsworth so hard that Debbie screamed and rushed forward, sobbing, to complain.

"It's the heat," sighed Cissie Updike. "It makes everybody cross. It makes a mean little kid even meaner. Here, Debbie, you want to push Carrington?"

"Oh, yes," said Debbie. Her face lit up. She dried her tears and took over the stroller from Cissie. Carrington rattled along happily, careless of the heat.

Georgie too was impervious to every kind of weather. But everybody else was miserable.

Eleanor looked for Sidney Bloom. "Listen, Sidney, how about a song or something?"

But Sidney was gray under his sunburn. "My feet hurt," he said.

"Didn't you bring another pair of shoes?"

"Oh, sure, but they're too small too. I guess my feet have grown." He took off one shoe and hopped along on the other foot, rubbing his toes.

Eleanor looked at his feet. They certainly were enormous.

By afternoon they were prostrated. They dragged themselves up a steep slope into a pine woods and flopped down in the shade, flat on their backs. Their thermoses were empty. They were parched.

When Oliver Winslow's sweaty red face heaved into sight, Frieda had a good idea. "Hey, Oliver," she said, sitting up, "go find us some water."

"Water?" said Oliver, grinning foolishly.

"That's right." Frieda waved her hand at wells and gushing fountains out there in the world somewhere. "Just go out there and get some and bring it back."

"Well, okay," said Oliver.

While he was gone, the rest of them lay gasping, batting at flies.

Eddy glanced at Eleanor. "Whatever happened to all those TV guys?" he said. "I thought we were going to be famous."

"They got bored with us, I guess," said Eleanor. And anyway, Eleanor thought dismally, how would anybody ever find them now? They weren't on Route 1 anymore, they were on some treadmill somewhere, some asphalt treadmill, trudging past the same shopping plazas and gasoline stations and motels and fast-food places, going around in circles. The whole country was covered with blacktop and broken glass and beer cans. "What the flag of my country means to me," whispered Eleanor to herself cynically.

There was a familiar clatter on the road. The Green Horror was back. They all gave a feeble cheer as Oliver staggered up the slope with two jugs of water he had found at the house of a local farmer. "It's from his own spring," said Oliver, as the cool water glugged into the first of the empty thermoses. "He pumps it into a tub in his attic."

They drank and drank the clear water and then stumbled back to the road.

Eleanor walked beside Georgie and looked at her sidelong, studying her. Georgie's face was drawn and thin. There were blue-milk circles under her eyes. And the flag drooping over her shoulder was nothing but a gray rag, like something picked up from the litter along the highway.

"Do you think we'll make it to Bridgeport today?" said Georgie anxiously.

"I don't know, Georgie. I sort of doubt it."

Eleanor fixed her eyes on a faraway tobacco barn. As they moved forward it seemed to stay fixed on the horizon. Slowly, slowly it shifted from front, to side, to rear. At this rate they would never get to Washington, D.C. They would never get anywhere.

And then Eleanor hit bottom. What was the use of going to Washington at all? Even if they actually got there, even if the President agreed to speak to Georgie, what good would that do? Georgie was too shy, too tongue-tied to talk to the President. And her letter wouldn't do any good either. It was just an ordinary little kid's fourth-grade letter. Eleanor had read it. It wasn't going to change the President's mind.

But nothing was ever so bad that it couldn't get worse. At the next rest stop everything fell apart.

It was a low place, lower than the road. A trickle of water flowed through a huge pipe under the highway and went gurgling into a concrete ditch that carried it farther down the hill. They all took off their hot shoes and paddled in the water. Then, while Eleanor groped in her knapsack, she was transfixed by a bloodcurdling scream.

It was Rachel Adzarian, stuck in the pipe.

Weezie Hoskins came out of the pipe, splashing in the stream, shrugging her shoulders, protesting loudly. "I didn't do anything. All I said was I saw a snake in the water. That's all I said."

Eleanor dropped her knapsack and ran to the pipe. Far under the road she could see the huddled shape of Rachel, cramped against the curving wall, her arms flung out on either side, her bare toes high and dry, her mouth open in scream after hideous scream.

It took two of them to get her out, Eleanor and Robert, half dragging, half carrying a frantic Rachel. And then when she was safely out in the open air, Rachel stopped shrieking about snakes and began shrieking about something worse, something much more terrible.

"I want to go home," sobbed Rachel. "I want to go home." She was blubbering it at the top of her lungs.

"Well, all right," said Eleanor. "You can go home. You can call your mother at the next gas station. It's *okay*, Rachel."

But now they were all crying, "Me, too." Rachel's homesickness was catching. "I want to go home. I want to go home." Feeble hands clutched at Eleanor and Frieda, at Cissie and Eddy. "I want to go home."

In a daze of heat and exhaustion, Eleanor tried to calm them down. She held out her hands and shouted at them. "Okay, okay, it's all right. If you want to go home, it's okay. You can call your parents at the next phone. Now just quiet down. Listen"—an uneasy queasy sensation gripped Eleanor—"how many of you feel that way? How many want to go home? Just raise your hands."

Then she winced and closed her eyes.

"Oh, wow," muttered Eddy, aghast.

"Oh, no," murmured Georgie, dismayed.

It was everybody. Well, almost everybody. Gray-faced fifth graders looked at each other blankly and lifted their dirty hands. The fourth graders deserted in a body with storms of weeping. They had been brave and good, so brave! so good! They had marched a hundred miles! But now they could march no longer. They wanted to leave the endlesss highway, the fumes of gasoline and diesel fuel, the ugly roar of hurtling cars. They wanted to go home, to be fed breakfast and lunch and supper, to be tucked into comfortable beds by loving mothers and fathers, far from the sordid margin of Route 1. Even Sidney Bloom was slowly raising his hand, his usually cheerful face wan and solemn.

It was a terrible moment. A sulphurous sense of nightmare hung over them. The place where they had stopped was like a shabby corner of hell, littered with nameless refuse. Toilet paper was tangled in the bushes in tattered streamers. Above them on the highway a huge truck was accelerating. The whine of its eighteen enormous tires screamed above the roar of its engine, grinding into their brains, raising the level of their wretchedness. Why were they here? What on earth were they doing in this weird and horrible place? Nobody could remember.

"Well, all right," said Eleanor, her voice cracking. "Okay, okay. It's all right." She exchanged a miserable glance with Frieda, and looked around for Robert.

Robert was leaning against the guardrail, gazing at the sky, ignoring the whole thing. Eleanor felt an additional twinge of irritation. She took out her package of Kleenex and passed it among the sobbing fourth graders. Frieda had a wet washcloth. She walked around, mopping faces, cooling burning foreheads. Cissie looked on, disconsolate, her arms folded on the push bar of the stroller, her damp hair stuck to her flushed cheeks. Even Carrington's pudgy face was sober.

Weezie Hoskins was the straw that nearly broke Eleanor's back. Weezie tugged at Eleanor and gazed up at her with her ratty little dirty face. "Do *I* have to go home? I want to stay with you."

"I'm not going home either," promised Oliver Winslow stoutly, clapping Eddy on the back.

Eleanor could feel her mouth quiver. The good kids were leaving, the scruffy ones were sticking fast. She kept her face forward as they took to the road again. Salt tears were running down her cheeks. She took Georgie's hand and squeezed it. Georgie squeezed back, but she didn't look up. Eleanor suspected Georgie was crying too. Her flag was raveled into nothing. It was a threadbare skeleton of itself.

The next stretch of highway was long. The sun beat down. Their feet dragged. Tears began to flow again. The careless traffic scuttled by.

"Hey, look," said Eddy, "there goes one of those TV vans, see? It says NBC."

Eleanor turned her head. The van was rushing past them. It didn't slow down. A moment later two more vans plunged down the road in the same direction.

"CBS and ABC," said Eddy.

Only the fourth van, the one from PBS, slowed down as it passed the straggling procession of children on the side of the road. Someone looked out as though he wanted to say something, but then the van speeded up again and raced away, charging after the others along Route 1.

The message could not have been clearer, thought Eleanor resentfully. The Children's Crusade wasn't news anymore. They were a lost cause. It was just as well. It would be embarrassing to have to confess to the whole world that the crusade had shriveled to almost nothing.

"I guess something must be happening in Bridgeport," said Eddy.

Eleanor laughed cynically. "Maybe Veronica Glassmore has called a press conference. Or maybe everybody in Bridgeport has joined the President's Flag Brigade." Bitterness racked Eleanor.

"Hey, look," said Frieda, "something's going on." She pointed at the overpass far down the road. "That must be the intersection with Interstate 95. Something's happening."

They stared at the distant highway bridge, trying to see what Frieda's big glasses saw. There was a streak across the road at that point. A lot of cars were pulled up, and several big yellow vehicles that looked like school buses.

"It's a whole lot of people," said Eddy, squinting, peering at the bridge. "Look, millions of them, all over the place."

"It must be a baseball game or something," said Eleanor. "A lot of people going to a game."

But the people weren't moving. They were just standing there, a mass of little jiggling blobs. The procession of discouraged crusaders struggled slowly forward, their eyes on the intersection, wondering what was going on. They were beginning to hear noises, a lot of high-pitched shouting.

"Maybe it's an accident," said Eddy. "Some gruesome twenty-car collision."

But there were no wrecked cars on the highway, no policemen stopping traffic, no flashing lights, no ambulances racing to the scene.

"Listen," said Cissie, "that noise, it's cheering. They're all cheering about something. See those balloons? They're letting them go. Look at them go!"

"I can see the TV vans," said Frieda, frowning. "There they are, all four of them. Something really important must be happening."

Eddy was awestruck. "There are so many people," he said. Then he stopped in his tracks. "Listen, I think it's—I think they're all—hey!" cried Eddy. "It's kids! It's all kids! They've got backpacks and balloons and signs! They're waiting for *us*! They're cheering for *us*!"

And in that instant the Pilgrimage of Peace, the Children's Crusade, Georgie's march to Washington, was reborn. It had almost died, but now it was alive again.

The news raced down the line. They all began running. Their tears were forgotten. Their homesickness was over, their weariness a thing of the past. Screaming with excitement, they galloped forward to meet the children who had walked from Hartford and Waterbury and Springfield and Poughkeepsie, who had come by bus from places too far for walking, from Illinois and Indiana and Kentucky and Tennessee. They were pelted with daisies and dandelions. Balloons sailed up in the air. Signs waggled up and down in sweaty hands:

MARTIN LUTHER KING
ELEMENTARY SCHOOL
BUFFALO, NEW YORK

JACKIE ROBINSON JUNIOR HIGH SCHOOL
HARLEM, NEW YORK

MRS. HUSSEY'S SIXTH GRADE CLASS
GEORGE W. PALMER
ELEMENTARY SCHOOL
JETHRO, ILLINOIS
PRESENT 100%!

It was wonderful. Cissie raced after Eddy and Frieda, dragging the stroller behind her, with

Carrington tossing and pitching under one arm. Eleanor ran too, feeling a flicker of dismay as she saw all the dirty tear-streaked faces rushing past her. She should have tried to clean them up. She should have made them comb their hair. Her own face was stiff with tearstained dirt, and the red eye of one of the television cameras was looking right at her. Eleanor laughed insanely and threw her arms around a girl with a sign that said:

NO NUKES!
BLEWETT ELEMENTARY SCHOOL
ST. LOUIS, MISSOURI

The rest of them, too, were wild with joy. Eleanor was astonished to see Rachel Adzarian hopping up and down, screeching with rapture. The snakes were forgotten, along with her desperate yearning for home. Sidney Bloom was playfully punching a boy from the Frances Willard Elementary School in Kansas City, and the boy was punching him back. Frieda was shrieking something about permission slips, and little pieces of paper were suddenly waggling in the air—permission slips, a thousand permission slips! Frieda threw back her head and screamed with laughter. And Georgie's stars and stripes were flying. She was dancing up and down beside Frieda. Eleanor looked at the flag, and couldn't believe her eyes. It was whole again. It was snapping and billowing. It was red and white and brilliant blue.

Gone was all thought of going home. The Children's Crusade was famous and successful. From now on they would be a marching mob, a thousand strong. Eleanor found Eddy and goggled at him joyfully and hugged him.

And then once again she was clutched by doubt. She cornered a cameraman. "The Flag Brigade," she shouted at him, "do they have a lot of kids too? Do you know how many they've got?"

"The what?"

"The President's Flag Brigade. A lot of other kids who support the President."

The cameraman looked puzzled. "Never heard of 'em."

"Really?"

"Hey, listen," said the cameraman, bellowing to make himself heard above the din—he was shaking his head in awe and smiling at Eleanor with admiration—"I got to hand it to you kids. It's crazy. They're doing it all over the world. You know, in France. The kids are marching on Paris. And London, and Amsterdam, and Bonn and New Delhi. I even heard a rumor they're marching on Moscow. Kids, just kids. It's some kind of global hysteria. You kids are really nuts."

But he was grinning. You could tell he was really impressed.

"All the Children in the World . . ."

— ☆ —

The President watched the progress of the Children's Crusade every evening on the television news. When the crusaders marched down the main street of Stamford, Connecticut, he saw the parade on the TV set in his sitting room on the second floor of the White House, in the company of his wife and Charley Chase.

Mobs of children filled the street. They were carrying signs:

> **FITZ-SIMMONS JUNIOR HIGH SCHOOL**
> **PHILADELPHIA, PA.**

> *LINCOLN ELEMENTARY SCHOOL*
> *MINNEAPOLIS, MINNESOTA*

> ## PONCE DE LEON JUNIOR HIGH SCHOOL
> ## ~~CORAL GABLES, FLORIDA~~

> ### *DOBIE JUNIOR HIGH SCHOOL*
> ### *AUSTIN, TEXAS*

> ## MRS. HUSSEY'S SIXTH GRADE CLASS
> ## GEORGE W. PALMER
> ## ELEMENTARY SCHOOL
> ## JETHRO, ILLINOIS
> ## PRESENT 100%!

In the middle of Stamford, in Veterans' Park, they stopped marching and a tough little kid with yellow pigtails gave a speech. Her small red face filled the screen. The Childen's Crusade had an official protest, she said, and their leader was going to hand it to the President in the White House. That was what they were going to do in Washington, D.C.—they were going to march to the White House to present their protest.

"Hey, I think she's kind of cute," said the President's wife.

"Cute like a charging rhinoceros," snickered Charley Chase.

Then Derek Cherniak's handsome face appeared on the screen. He stood against a background of marching children and gave an excited report about the world movement against the Peace Missile. "In the United Nations the debate goes on. In Nevada a large group of mothers continues to camp beside the entrance to the launching platform. In London's Grosvenor Square great crowds of angry Londoners are assembled outside the American Embassy. In Rome the Pope appeared today before a vast multitude jammed into St. Peter's Square to pray for a change of heart on the part of the President of the United States. In Tokyo two million signatures have been collected against the Peace Missile. In San Francisco teams of scientists are working around the clock to prove that the new weapon will endanger the earth. But so far nothing has changed the President's determination to launch the missile."

Derek Cherniak's face was usually calm and serene. But now his eyes blinked nervously, and he stuttered, as he said that the last hope against the Peace Missile was the international movement called the Children's Crusade. "They are marching to Washington, to Ottawa, to Mexico City, to London, to Paris, to Bonn, to Stockholm, to Copenhagen, to Rome, to Madrid, to Tokyo, to Canberra, to Moscow. Sometimes it seems as if all the children in the world are on the move."

Gloomily President Toby switched off the television set. For a moment he sat in silence with his wife and Charley Chase. Then he turned to Charley. "What did that little kid mean when she said they had a leader? Which one of those little ragamuffins is the leader?"

"I don't know," said Charley Chase. He slapped his knee and stood up. "I'll find out and let you know."

Next morning the President shut himself up alone in the Oval Office. It was very quiet in the office. Out there in the city of Washington a lot was going on. The President was perfectly aware that seven hundred and fifty thousand people inhabited the city, and that they were all on the move, going about their daily business. But he felt alone on the face of the earth. Alone except for a swarm of children coming his way, getting closer and closer, their faces turned toward him, demanding something of him. *All the children in the world are on the move.*

He could feel in his bones the light tread of their feet, shaking the pavement of Route 1 in Connecticut. Soon they would be marching through New York City and New Jersey and Pennsylvania and Maryland, and before long they would be trampling the lawn around the White House, and the pressure of their slight bodies would vibrate in the supporting timbers of the west wing, and shiver in the draperies at the window. Already President Toby could feel it trembling in the frames of his glasses, and quivering in the plates of his skull.

The President sank his head into his hands. For the first time during his term in office, he was afraid.

If only the marching columns approaching the White House were a throng of grown men and women, a million strong, then he would know what to do. He would simply ignore them, and sooner or later they would go away.

And if it were an assaulting army of tanks and guns, that, too, would be easy to handle. The Air Force would destroy them with strafing planes and fighter bombers. The Army would bombard them with artillery. The Navy would send in the Marines.

But it wasn't grown men and women. It wasn't an army of guns and tanks. It was *children, a thousand children.* And they were the most dangerous army of all.

You couldn't argue with them, that was the trouble. It would be like talking to Robert. Last May the President had tried to explain things to his own grandson, without any success at all.

"Why don't you talk to the Russians?" Robert had said. "Why don't you just sit down and talk the whole thing over? And then both sides could agree to throw away all their nuclear weapons. You know, on both sides."

Poor deluded boy. He just didn't understand the complexities, the difficulties. When, for example, was this conversation with the Soviets supposed to take place? You couldn't possibly sit down and talk to them when you were *behind* them in nuclear strength. You had to catch up first in order to have any bargaining power at all. And if you were *ahead* of them, the result of talking things over wouldn't be fair—*you* would be the only one who would be giving up weapons, not the Russians. Surely no sensible person would want that to happen.

But children couldn't understand that sort of high-level logic. Children were only children. They didn't know the complexities and dangers of the real world.

And then the President remembered something from long ago. For a moment he was a child again himself, back home in Twin Falls, Idaho, that little one-horse town on the Snake River, where he had grown up. The Tobys had been a churchgoing, Bible-reading family. Young James had learned hundreds of Bible verses by heart. Now one of the verses came back to him, unbidden. *Verily I say unto you, except ye turn, and become as little children, ye shall in no wise enter the Kingdom. . . .*

Except ye turn, and become as little children . . . The President gasped and clutched his desk and stood up, wrenching at his collar.

There was a knock at the door.

It was Charley Chase. The President strode forward to take his hand. He was relieved to see him. The very presence of Charley Chase was a comfort. At once the President was surrounded by the old set of opinions he shared with Charley. Once again the room was the Oval Office, not a Sunday school back there in Twin Falls, Idaho. It was a center for decisive action, for calm planning, for the sharing of common beliefs. In the company of Charley Chase the President was no longer shaken by doubt.

"I've been in touch with young Veronica Glassmore," said Charley importantly. "She gave me an earful on the inner workings of the Children's

Crusade. The real leader is one of the younger children, a little kid named Georgie Hall. A shy youngster, I gather, but Veronica says she's right at the hard core of the whole thing. And she's got a flag, an old American flag that seems to be the inspiration for the whole crusade. Now, listen here—I've got an idea. If we could just lay our hands on that flag, the entire march would lose its rallying point, its central symbol."

"Surely one single flag wouldn't make that much difference?" said the President.

"Oh, yes, it could. Veronica was very strong on that point. 'That flag,' she said, 'it's really important. You've got to get rid of the flag.' "

"Well, surely," said the President mildly, "that shouldn't be too difficult?"

Where Is Robert Toby?

— ☆ —

Across the highway as they entered the new town there was a huge banner:

**LARCHMONT, NEW YORK,
SALUTES
THE CHILDREN'S CRUSADE**

"Here we go again," said Eddy, striding along with Sidney behind half a dozen New York state troopers on motorcycles. He grinned at Sidney. "You can't even hear yourself think."

The street was lined with cheering people. And in Flint Park, waiting beside the picnic tables with their platters of hot dogs and pizza and brownies and root beer, stood the new recruits, complete with permission slips, backpacks and sleeping bags, jeans, flashlights, sunburn lotion, stamped postcards, and first-aid kits for emergency use in the field.

"Permission slips, please?" said Frieda, putting first things first.

For Eleanor the march had become a nightmare. She had no privacy. She couldn't rush off into the woods in search of a Big Tree without running into a cameraman. Crawling into her sleeping bag at night she never knew whether or not a telephoto lens was focused on her. And since she was one of the tallest crusaders, she was always finding a microphone under her nose.

"Can you tell me, Miss, the fundamental goals and purposes of the Children's Crusade?"

"Oh, you'll have to talk to Frieda Caldwell," Eleanor would say sternly. "She's the Media Interface Person."

And then Frieda would jerk a piece of paper out of her new dime-store briefcase, her fact sheet on *The Fundamental Goals and Purposes of the Children's Crusade*.

Frieda had fact sheets on everything. She had typed them up and photocopied them in a church in Westport, Connecticut. One of her fact sheets—or rather, a whole sheaf of fact sheets—listed the names, addresses, telephone numbers, ages, and schools of all the marchers. She was continually in motion up and down the line, updating the list, recording the new recruits. Frieda was a demon for organization.

Both Georgie and Eleanor were astonished by what had happened to Frieda. Her ordinary nine-year-old bossiness had swollen to fit the crisis. She was amazing. She was a titanic leader. She had set up a system of captains to patrol the flank of the march to keep anybody from running out into the road, and another system of captains to meet every night to discuss problems that had come up during the day. She had made herself a mega-phone by knocking the bottom out of a popcorn container, and it worked fine. The popcorn megaphone and Frieda were inseparable. She was always shouting "NOW HEAR THIS" through the megaphone and explaining a new rule.

"NOW HEAR THIS! EVERYBODY HAS TO STAY IN THE SAME PLACE IN LINE. NO CHANGING PLACES. CAPTAINS, PLEASE DECIDE THE ORDER OF MARCH IN YOUR PART OF THE LINE, SO WE KNOW WHERE EVERYBODY IS ALL THE TIME AND WE DON'T LOSE ANYBODY, OKAY?"

"NOW HEAR THIS! CAPTAINS WILL PLEASE APPOINT AN OFFICIAL BAG PER-SON FOR THEIR OWN PEOPLE, OKAY?"

"NOW HEAR THIS! ANYBODY WHO GETS SICK CAN RIDE IN THE RED CROSS VEHICLE AT THE END OF THE LINE, BUT YOUR CAPTAIN HAS TO SAY IT'S OKAY, OKAY? THIS IS A MARCH, NOT A RIDE IN A ROLLS-ROYCE, RIGHT?"

"Rolls-Royce?" laughed Sidney. "She means the Green Horror."

"Red Cross vehicle?" snickered Eddy. "They'll get sick just from riding in it. I'll bet it's got typhoid germs in the upholstery."

Georgie was pleased with all the new rules and arrangements. Whatever Frieda did was all right with Georgie. Whenever Frieda was busy running things, walking backward along the line, shouting orders, Georgie marched with Eleanor. The rest of the time she marched with Frieda, so that her best friend could have a rest from her enormous responsibilities.

But Eleanor sometimes felt resentful about the way Frieda had taken over. She scolded herself for feeling that way. After all, somebody had to run things. Georgie couldn't do it. She wasn't an organizer. And Eleanor herself was too old.

And anyway, Eleanor had her own responsibilities. She wasn't doing important things like working out the marching arrangements with the New York City Police Department, or talking to the press. Nothing sensational or glamorous like that. Eleanor was stuck with the baby-sitting detail. All the whiniest of the younger children came flocking to Eleanor. Her sheer size made them seek her out, the way baby chicks gather around a hen. There were always two or three grubby little kids clinging to her, their fists knotted in her shirt, or twisted in the straps of her knapsack. It was like dragging a lot of extra baggage. It was as though she moved in a cloud of sticky fingers, dirty faces, whimpering voices, dusty T-shirts, dirty knees. She felt like one of those monkeys that carry their young on their backs, or a mother spider with millions of portable offspring. Every few minutes some pint-sized person would tug at her, to show her a sore elbow, or complain about some injustice.

"I gave Linda Fink my ice cream cone to hold, and she ate it," wept Debbie McGregor from Hartford, Connecticut.

"But it was melting!" exclaimed Linda Fink from Great Barrington, Massachusetts.

The youngest marcher had a wad of gum stuck in her hair. "Weezie," said Eleanor in horrified surprise, "what's this? Good grief." And then she had to cut it out, after Frieda bawled through the megaphone, "SCISSORS? WHO'S GOT A PAIR OF SCISSORS?"

All day, every day, Eleanor solved problems and bolstered up the weakest, while Frieda, the strongest, flexed her wiry muscles and shouted through her megaphone.

As the swarms of marchers grew larger and larger, Robert Toby grew more and more invisible. Even on Frieda's official list he didn't exist. There was someone named Robert Thompson on the list, but no Robert Toby. At first the new kids always looked at Robert curiously, but then they accepted his name and admired the Buckeyes and Angel Wings pinned to the cotton in his specimen box.

"Where were you this time?" said Eddy, when Robert suddenly joined him again after the grand march down Fifth Avenue in New York City.

"Oh, I was just hacking around," said Robert.

"You didn't find any butterflies in the middle of New York!"

Robert thought a minute. "How about in Central Park?"

As for Cissie Updike, she too had suddenly burgeoned and magnified and assumed importance, just like Frieda. Cissie had become a kind of queen, with a court of ladies-in-waiting. As the older sister of Carrington, she was lionized and besieged. Everyone wanted to push Carrington's stroller. Regally, Cissie decided whose turn it was now, and whose turn after that. But she wasn't fair. Some people had more turns than others. There were angry accusations and arguments. One frustrated Carrington-pusher came to Eleanor in a rage. Her name was Elizabeth Hotchkiss. Elizabeth was from Gary, Indiana. "Amanda took my turn," cried Elizabeth. "Amanda already *had* a turn."

Eleanor sighed, and walked back along the line to investigate. She hadn't seen Cissie and Carrington for days.

She found the two of them at the end of the procession, surrounded by admirers and handmaidens. One of the smaller girls was bowed under the weight of Cissie's backpack as well as her own. Somebody else was carrying Bingo. One lucky nursemaid was pushing Carrington's stroller. Carrington himself was jiggling along comfortably, his mouth open, his eyes closed, sound asleep on the road. His big sister pranced along beside him, free of encumbrances. She was wearing a blazing white tennis dress, clean white tennis shoes, and little white socks with pompoms on the back.

"Hey," said Eleanor, "where did you get that outfit?"

"In New Brunswick," said Cissie airily. "I bought it with my own money."

"They're paying her," said Elizabeth Hotchkiss

angrily. "She's got lots of money. They're paying her a quarter apiece to push Carrington."

"So?" said Cissie defiantly. "What's the matter with that? He's *my* little brother. If they want to pay me, why should I say no?"

Eleanor looked at Cissie's new clothes with distaste. "You look terrible," she said truthfully. "Really terrible. You know, like a fashion model or something, not like a pilgrim on an important crusade."

"Don't worry," said Elizabeth sarcastically. "She won't look like that very long."

And of course Elizabeth was right. Pretty soon Cissie's glaring white dress was coated with a fine gray film, just like all the jeans and shorts and T-shirts in the line. She blended right in with everybody else.

Whenever Eleanor could escape her duties as problem solver and substitute mother, she made friends with the new marchers. Some of them had made journeys as heroic as that of the original band from Concord. One batch of recruits who had joined them in New York City were already seasoned travelers. Fifty-five of them had taken a bus from Atlanta to Philadelphia, and then they had walked the ninety miles to New York. Now they were retracing their steps through the evil-smelling New Jersey landscape of oil refineries and enormous storage tanks and tall pipes blazing with waste gas.

"How can you stand walking through it twice?" said Eleanor, waving her hand at a wrecked-automobile lot, where cars that had been crushed into cubes were heaped in hideous piles.

"Oh, we don't mind," said a boy from Eudora, Georgia. He smiled at Eleanor. "It sure is in a good cause."

And then Eleanor felt hopeful. She liked their southern voices. After their soft drawling sentences that ran smoothly together, her own words sounded to her like green snaps of celery, chopped off into bites.

Slowly, slowly, the Children's Crusade marched through New Jersey and across the southeastern corner of Pennsylvania. When it crossed the line into Maryland, the pace picked up. They began to feel the excitement of approaching their goal. They were *getting there.*

On the way to Baltimore, Frieda shouted through her popcorn megaphone: "NOW HEAR THIS! THERE WILL BE AN IMPORTANT MEETING OF CAPTAINS AFTER SUPPER IN BALTIMORE, OKAY? CAPTAINS, DO YOU HEAR ME? PASS IT ALONG!"

The meeting of the captains was held in the Holy Redeemer Cemetery, a Baltimore burying ground belonging to the Catholics, the same good people who had provided the marchers with an enormous smörgasbord supper earlier in the evening. Now all the members of the Children's Crusade were spread out among the gravestones.

"What," demanded Frieda, "is going to happen when we get there? I mean, I think we'd better decide what we're really, really going to do, right?"

They sat silent, struck dumb at the thought of actually being required to accomplish the purpose for which they had set out. Then all heads turned to look at Georgie. Georgie wasn't a captain, but she was an honorary member of the committee.

Georgie flushed, and wrapped one hand in her flag. "I just want to give my letter to the President," she said.

There was another pause.

Then Eleanor spoke up. "It isn't what *we* do, it's what they'll *let* us do," she said.

"That's right," said Eddy. "We have to know that first. Suppose they won't let anybody into the White House at all? Or suppose they won't even let us come into the city of Washington in the first place?"

"I wish there were some way we could find out what they're going to do," said a boy from Minneapolis. "We really need to know, if we're going to make a plan of action."

"That's right." The other captains were all nodding their heads.

"What do *you* think, Robert?" said Frieda sharply, staring at Robert Toby. Robert was standing to one side of the ring of committee members, staring at a polished ball on the top of a marble obelisk. He glanced at Frieda, then looked back at the ball. "Don't ask me," he said, hunching his shoulders. "I don't know."

"Hey, listen," said Oliver Winslow, "I'll tell you what I think we should do."

Oliver wasn't a captain, so of course he shouldn't have been at the meeting, but Frieda was lenient. She needed help wherever she could get it. "Okay, Oliver, what do you think?"

"I think we should call ahead to the next town every day. You know, from a phone booth, and tell them we like pizza and spaghetti and ice cream." Oliver gestured scornfully at his second helping of raspberry gelatin. "You know, like they could be the official food of the pilgrimage, okay? I mean, if people are going to cook a lot of food, they might as well cook something we like, right?"

Eleanor was horrified. "Oh, Oliver, that's a terrible idea."

"Hey, look," said Sidney Bloom, "if we're going to have some kind of official food, I think it should be chile con carne and chocolate cake."

There was a chorus of disagreement. Tracy Chin from Boston wanted tacos. Petie Badger from Chicago suggested steak. Diane O'Brien from Schenectady was homesick for old-fashioned meat loaf and baked potatoes.

"Hey, I know," shouted Sidney, "why don't we ask for different things every day?"

There was a burst of applause at this suggestion, and Sidney promptly jumped to his feet and put it in the form of a motion.

"STOP, STOP, SHUT UP, LISTEN," screamed Eleanor. She had to jump up, too, and shake Sidney. "You can't, you just can't." Then Eleanor made a speech about how generous the people in the towns had been, and how the Children's Crusade would seem fussy and spoiled and rotten if they demanded some particular kind of food, and, anyway, wasn't it always delicious? Shouldn't they just be grateful? "Who do we think we are, anyway?" concluded Eleanor, and sat down, her face red.

There was silence for a minute, as the captains

came to their senses, and then Oliver's insane suggestion was voted down.

It was time for bed. The Concord marchers wandered around the cemetery and picked out a cool breezy corner on a little rise, with pink marble tombstones. In her weariness, Eleanor saw the tombstones as the heads of cozy beds. She unrolled her sleeping bag in front of one, and settled down for the night. Georgie stuck her flagstaff firmly in the ground and snuggled down beside her.

In the middle of the night Eleanor woke up to see Eddy's flashlight poking around among the gravestones. "What are you doing, Eddy?" whispered Eleanor.

"Have you seen Robert?" said Eddy.

"Robert? No, not since the captains' meeting."

"Well, he must be around someplace," said Eddy.

But in the morning, Robert was nowhere to be found. When the march formed up along the iron fence of the cemetery, Robert did not come sauntering up to walk beside Eddy.

And Oliver Winslow too had decamped. The Green Horror was no longer parked beside the cemetery gate.

Eleanor felt betrayed. She didn't care about Oliver, but Robert's departure really hurt. "I know why he left," she said unhappily. "Don't forget, he's the President's grandson. I'll bet he was just a spy for the other side, the whole time."

"What do you mean?" said Eddy angrily. "That's stupid. Robert wouldn't do anything like that."

"Well, I don't know," said Eleanor. "Why didn't he say good-bye, or give some reason for going away? There's something fishy about it. Very fishy." And then her heart sank. "Listen, you know how Robert always ran away when anybody was taking pictures? You know why? Because he didn't want anybody in the country to think he was on our side. That's why. Because he really wasn't. He's been on the President's side, all along."

Eddy was silent. Eleanor could see that the force of her argument had hit home. She felt sick. Robert a traitor? It was hard to believe. Robert just didn't seem to be that kind of person. And yet, where was he? Why had he disappeared without a word?

Frieda blew a blast on her whistle and waved her arm. The whistle was brand-new, a gift from a traffic policeman in Newark. The Maryland state troopers kicked their big bikes into noisy life. The long weaving line of children started forward slowly. Soon they were stretched out at the side of the road in a straggling line a mile long.

Eleanor marched beside Georgie, left foot, right foot, left foot, right foot, swinging along easily with the rolling gait of an experienced pilgrim on the highways of the world. Georgie's flag caught the breeze and lifted gallantly and streamed behind them. The day's march had begun.

But where was Robert? Oh, where was Robert Toby?

Robert Turns Up

— ☆ —

"The rockbound coast of Maine," said the new flag bearer, reading his winning letter to the President, "that's what I always think of when I look at the American flag. And I think of the farmers in Aroostook County digging potatoes, and the lumberjacks along the Penobscot River cutting timber, and lonely lighthouse keepers keeping watch over the shipping in Casco Bay. And I think of moose browsing in the big woods, and beavers building their dams across our streams. . . ."

The new flag bearer was a boy named Harper Flint, a seventh grader from Orono, Maine. Harper and the President were sitting across from each other on the white sofas in the Oval Office.

The President enjoyed these sessions with the letter-writing winners. They were refreshing distractions from the heavy cares of his job. And he liked the lift it gave his spirits to catch a glimpse of one of the home states of the young flag bearers. Of course he had known the geography of the country ever since he himself had been a child, but lately he was getting a new view of the broad nation. It was as though these young people were filling in great blank spaces on the map with detail. New cities loomed on the horizon, new mountain peaks, new lakes and winding rivers, new fields of growing corn. He was coming to feel affection for every corner of the land.

"Thank you, Harper," said the President, when his new flag bearer at last lowered his sheet of paper.

But Harper wasn't finished. "And sir, wouldn't it be wonderful," he said quickly, "if all of us there in Orono could look up at the stars and not worry about—"

"That will do, Harper," said the President, holding up his hand.

"Yes, sir," said Harper Flint, turning red.

"You can be excused now. Mrs. Colefax will tell you about your first assignment. Thank you, Harper. Don't forget to take the flag."

"Oh, no, sir," said Harper. Plucking the glittering God-Bless-America flag from its stand beside the fireplace, he left the Oval Office and went back to his room on the third floor of the White House.

The President spent the next hour with Charley Chase. Their conference was something like the meeting of the captains of the Children's Crusade in the cemetery in Baltimore. It was a planning session.

"What the heck are we going to do when those little kids get here?" Charley wanted to know.

"I don't know, Charley," said the President, shaking his head sadly. "What *are* we going to do?"

"Well, as a matter of fact, I do have a suggestion for something you should do right now, before they arrive. You should make another television address. Only this time you bring in the young people—your grandson Robert and some of the kids who have been flag bearers so far, like this new kid Harper Flint. You could all sit down together, like in a family council. You'd be showing your sympathy for the younger generation. You could talk over the international situation together. Explain your side of things. Show that you care what they think."

The President looked drawn and anxious. "Good," he said. "As long as we have a script. I don't want to take a chance that any of those children might pipe up with something—ah—

unexpected." The President looked at his watch. "Look, you see if you can get hold of a couple of the earlier flag bearers, Maria Verdade or DuBose Boudreau or David Klein. I'll call Robert's mother. She could pick him up at school right now, and put him on the ten o'clock plane."

But the President's daughter-in-law was staggered by his phone call.

"What do you mean, you want Robert to visit you? Robert isn't here in Concord. Robert is with you!"

"With me? Why, Alice, I haven't seen Robert since the middle of last month. What do you mean?"

"You haven't seen him? But he's been calling me from the White House for the last five and a half weeks!" Robert's mother was dismayed. "Do you mean he hasn't been telling me the truth? How terrible! Where can that boy be?"

"Now, Alice, don't upset yourself. If he's been calling you, he must be all right. I suggest you wait until he calls again, and then pin his ears back, and find out where on earth he is."

But at that very moment Robert was about to turn up. He was climbing out of a green Chevy Impala beside the locked gate of the White House on East Executive Avenue.

"Thanks, Oliver," said Robert, reaching for his

backpack. "I'll meet you here at noon, right?"

"Right," said Oliver, grinning, waving his hat. "So long."

Robert knocked at the door of the little house where one of the guards was on duty. "Hi, Jimmy," he said. "I'm back. Are you going to let me in?"

"Well, hi there, Robert," said the guard heartily. "Where you been? You look like you been through the war."

"Field trip," said Robert, flourishing his butterfly net.

"Oh, I get it," said the guard, clattering open the gate.

"Field trip," said Robert again to his grandfather in the Oval Office, dumping his knapsack on the yellow carpet. "Want to see my specimens?"

"Field trip?" The President was flabbergasted. He burst out laughing. "Oh, *butterflies.*"

Robert unbuckled the front pocket of his backpack and took out his specimen box. Opening it carefully, he displayed his collection. "I saw an Olive Hairstreak in a cedar pasture in Connecticut," said Robert, "but it got away."

"Now, listen here, young man," said the President firmly, "why didn't you tell your mother what you were up to?" He pointed at the telephone. "You call her right now. She's worried sick."

Robert's mother was relieved, but she was angry at the same time.

Robert listened patiently while she bawled him out. "I'm sorry," he said.

"Don't you ever do anything like that again!"

"I won't," said Robert.

Then he sat down with his grandfather and listened, while the President described the televised Family Council and Robert's part in it. "I want to explain to the children of the country why it's so important for the United States to put this missile up there in outer space. Can I count on you, Robert?"

Robert looked down at his worn sneakers. Then he shook his head. "No," he said. "I guess I don't want to do that."

"You don't want to do it?" The President couldn't believe it. "Whyever not? Because you're too bashful, is that it?" The President put his hands on Robert's shoulders and looked at him severely. "Now, Robert, you've got to get over that."

But Robert held firm. His grandfather scolded and pleaded. At last the President gave up, and sank back in his chair, bewildered.

Robert picked up his backpack. "Will it be okay

if I hang around your office this morning? I mean, could I just sort of sit in the corner?"

"Hang around?"

"Well, I'd sort of like to watch the way you work. You know, I'd like to see the administration of the whole country in action. I'd just like to understand what happens."

The President was pleased. "Well, of course, I'd be proud to have you here with me, Robert. I'm glad to see you interested in something more important than butterflies. As it turns out, some very big things are under discussion this morning. The missile launching, for instance. And the problem of what to do about this ragtag mob of children. I think you'll find it an interesting morning. But might I suggest— Tell me, Robert, when did you last have a bath?"

Robert's room was on the third floor of the White House, next to the one set aside for the flag bearer. Robert took a shower and changed his clothes—even his cleanest ones were gray with ground-in dirt—and went back out into the corridor. There he found Harper Flint wandering up and down, looking for the elevator. Harper was carrying the Presidential flag. His face was clouded with anxiety.

Robert introduced himself and led the way to

the stairs. On the way down, Harper confessed his inner turmoil.

"I feel really terrible. The telephone rang in my room just now. It was Mr. Chase. He wanted me to join your grandfather for a talk on television. And I said no."

At the bottom of the stairs Robert turned and led the way to the west wing. "You said no?"

"That's right. Oh, it would be such an honor, I know that. I was really flattered to be asked. It's just that I agree with the crusade. You know"— Harper glanced sideways at Robert—"the Children's Crusade. All those kids marching to Washington. I'm really sorry."

"Oh, it's okay," said Robert. "I don't mind."

Then Harper cleared his throat and stiffened his grip on his gold-spangled flag and revealed his darkest secret. "I'm going to march with them," he told Robert. "When they get to Washington I'm going to walk right out of the White House and join the Children's Crusade. I'm sorry, but that's what I'm going to do." Harper's jaw clenched with determination.

Robert gave him a dazzling smile. "Well, good for you," he said.

The President was deep in discussion with Charley Chase when Robert appeared in the doorway of the Oval Office. "Is it okay if Harper Flint comes in too?" said Robert.

Charley Chase looked doubtful and shook his head at the President.

"Sorry, Robert, no," said the President. "Tell him to come back at four o'clock. I'll need him then. I'm going to sign a bill, and there'll be a lot of senators and congressmen on hand." Then as Robert came into the room and stood beside the fireplace, the President grinned at Charley Chase, who was raising his eyebrows. "Oh, don't worry about Robert. My grandson doesn't care about anything but butterflies and insects. He's a budding entomologist."

Robert stared fixedly at the ship models on the mantel.

The subject under discussion was the Children's Crusade.

"Well, as I was saying," murmured Charley Chase, "you remember our discussion about the flag."

"The flag?" said the President. "What flag?"

"That little girl's flag. You know, that little kid who's the heart and soul of the whole crusade. Young Veronica told us we had to get our hands on that little girl's flag. Well, I've got a couple of Secret Service men assigned to the job." Charley patted his knees smartly in a gesture of accomplishment. "It's all set. They're going to do the trick tomorrow morning. So that's taken care of. Now, as for the little kid herself—I think, judging from what Veronica had to say, we'd better make sure the child doesn't get into this building at all. We'll post extra guards at all the doors the day after tomorrow."

"The day after tomorrow? You mean—"

"Right, the Fourth of July. They're arriving on the Fourth of July. Now, let's talk about traffic control. I've been talking to the Chief of the Capital Police. He tells me there are four thousand more kids joining forces with the first group somewhere south of Baltimore."

"Four thousand more?" The President was horrified. "How many is that all together?"

"Eight thousand, so far."

"Eight thousand? Good heavens! Excuse me, Robert, did you say something?"

"Me? No, sir. I just coughed, that's all."

A Flamboyant Display
of Old Glory

— ☆ —

The meeting in the little town of Harwood Park, Maryland, of the four thousand original marchers and the four thousand new ones was a wild affair. It was like colliding avalanches, converging stampedes of buffalo.

And then, just a few miles farther on, in Waterloo, another five thousand appeared out of nowhere, unheralded and unexpected. They came from the far west, from California and Oregon and the state of Washington, from the Dakotas and Montana and Wyoming. Their existence had been rumored, then forgotten, then reported as a solemn fact, and then denied. Now they were here in the flesh, a grubby multitude of boisterous new pilgrims.

Frieda nearly lost her voice, screaming through her megaphone, blowing her whistle, trying to restore order.

At last she had everyone on the road. They were spread out, twelve abreast, all over the southbound lane of Route 1, a milling throng, marching behind a pair of slow-moving Maryland state police cruisers, while the northbound lane was opened to two-way traffic, with troopers walking backward in the middle, waving at the cars with sweeping gestures, shrilling their whistles.

Georgie marched with Eleanor, holding her flag high, while Sidney walked in front of them, facing the procession, leading the singing.

I been working on the railroad,

sang Georgie, her eyes glowing,

All the livelong day.

Behind her the song washed backward through the thirteen thousand pilgrims. By the time it reached the last row, Sidney was starting another song at the front.

We shall over-co-o-ome,

sang Georgie,

We shall over-co-o-ome,
We shall overcome! some! day-ay-ay-ay-ay!

She was in a fever of excitement. Everything was going well. It was going to be all right. Her letter had been waiting in her knapsack for weeks, squeezed down in the very bottom, but now at last she was going to give it to the President. He would read it, and then he would understand. He would know what to do.

Eleanor was sick to death of being a nurserymaid. When the floodtide of new marchers joined them at Waterloo, she called it quits. It was impossible. There were far too many little kids. If they had problems, they would just have to take care of them by themselves. Why hadn't they stayed at home in the first place?

But of course she couldn't give up. Fretful children clustered around her in greater numbers than before. It was worse than ever.

A boy from Indiana had hiccups. "They won't (*c'CUP!*) stop (*c'CUP!*)" he said.

"I've got a cure for that. And it always works." Eleanor looked at him solemnly and then suddenly she let out a shriek.

The boy gasped. His hiccups stopped. "Gee, thanks," he said, smiling with relief. "That was really neat."

A girl from New Hampshire had a similar problem. "*Aa-aa-CHOO,*" she said, helplessly wiping her streaming eyes. "By doze is all stuffed up, ad I have to sdeeze. *Aa-CHOO.*"

"You're probably allergic to something growing beside the road," said Eleanor. She pulled a bandanna out of her knapsack. "Here, tie this around your face and see if it helps."

The poor girl sneezed five times while she was fastening the bandanna, but then she seemed better.

"Gee, thagks," said the girl. "I thig it's stopped."

"You look like a burglar," giggled Eleanor.

On the outskirts of Maryland City, the road dipped in a long hollow, then rose again. At the top of the rise Eleanor turned to look back. From there she could see the entire marching horde at once, all thirteen thousand of them, a vast profusion of bobbing heads and sunburned shoulders. She had never seen so many people all together at one time. Her throat filled with thick tears and she sobbed.

When she turned around, Robert was walking beside her. On the other side of the highway Oliver Winslow was opening the trunk of the Green Horror.

"Oh, Robert," wept Eleanor, "where have you been?"

"With my grandfather," said Robert.

"I thought so," said Eleanor. "I thought so."

But Robert had something else on his mind.

"Listen," he said, "we've got to hide Georgie's flag. She mustn't carry it openly like that any longer. He's going to kidnap it. He's going to try to steal it." Robert turned to look down at Georgie. "Here, Georgie, give it to me. We'll take it off the pole and hide it in somebody's backpack."

"He's going to steal it?" Eleanor was astonished. "You mean your *grandfather* is going to steal it?"

"Oh, no, not my grandfather. Somebody in the Secret Service." Robert held out his hand for Georgie's flag. "Come on, Georgie, let me have it."

But Georgie wouldn't give it up. She looked at them defiantly.

"It's okay, Georgie," said Eleanor. "I'll fold it up and hide it safely in my own backpack."

It was no use. Georgie was adamant. She clung to the mop handle and wouldn't let go. Her face was set in her stubborn expression of absolute determination. There was to be no separating Georgie from the fragile banner she had carried from the beginning, from Concord to Providence, from Providence to New Haven, from New Haven to New York, from New York to Philadelphia, from Philadelphia to this very stretch of asphalt on the road to Washington. She was nearly there—only one more day!—and she wasn't about to give up her precious burden.

"Oh, well, never mind," said Robert. His face was blank again, with his old faraway inattentive look. "It'll be okay."

"Okay? What do you mean, okay?" Eleanor was beside herself. "We can't let them do that to Georgie."

"No, no, it will be all right," murmured Robert. "I've got another idea." Then he walked away from Eleanor and went looking for Frieda, leaving Georgie still clinging to her flag.

Frieda was experimenting with a brand-new gadget Oliver had found in a discount store in Washington. It was a walkie-talkie. She was trying it out, communicating with one of her captains down the line. "FRIEDA HERE, SIGNING OFF," she said loudly when she saw Robert. "Hey, Robert, this thing is great."

"Listen," said Robert, "there's a huge park down the road, right beside a factory. Oliver and I, we passed it in the car. It would be a good place for a rest stop, okay? I mean, it was a really big park."

"Good idea," said Frieda. She clicked on her walkie-talkie and spoke into it expertly. "FRIEDA HERE. NOW HEAR THIS . . ."

The park was only a mile down the road. It

was broad and spacious, surrounding the factory and running up into a low woods of oak and pine. There were picnic tables and a wishing well. There were ducks in a pond surrounded by white-painted stones.

With shouts of relief, the Children's Crusade drifted off the road into the park. They swarmed around the pond and tossed leftover bits of sandwiches to the ducks. They moved up the hill into the woods in search of a thousand big trees. They took off their shoes and sat on the grass.

And then Eleanor noticed the name of the factory, and she laughed. It was painted in giant block letters the entire length of the huge windowless building:

EAGLE FLAG COMPANY

She watched, as Robert wandered around the building, looking for the door. She knew what he was going to do.

Half an hour later he came out again, his arrangements complete. He had persuaded the management to demonstrate its generosity to the Children's Crusade, that internationally famous army of patriotic young citizens, celebrated throughout the world for their courageous journey, heroes and heroines who had appeared on television, who had inspired the children of all nations to join their historic pilgrimage.

After Robert's fine speech, the president of the flag company had been eager to lend a hand. "Help yourself, young man," he had said. "It's all yours." Before long the thirteen thousand pilgrims were flowing out onto the highway once again behind the ranked cruisers of the Maryland State Police. Five hundred of them were carrying bright new American flags. They were ordinary flags. They didn't sparkle or shine or shed glitter on the road. Two were lashed jauntily to the push bar of Carrington's stroller. Tiny flags fluttered from the shoulder straps of a thousand knapsacks. It was a forest of flags, a flamboyant display of Old Glory, a resplendent pageant of red, white, and blue.

One Simple
Tremendous Truth

— ☆ —

Charley Chase was apologetic. "I'm sorry, sir. I suppose you know what happened."

"All those flags?" The President laughed. His laughter was slightly hysterical. He couldn't stop. Coughing and choking, he tried to control himself. "I certainly do know what happened. What are we going to do now? There isn't even going to be a television chat, for lack of any children who want to chat with me." The President was feeling resentful. "Even Robert has let me down, my own grandson. He's gone again. I had to call his mother and get her all upset."

"Look at it this way, sir," said Charley. "By tomorrow night it will be all over." He hitched forward on the sofa and began ticking things off on his fingers. "Here's the schedule for tomorrow. Early in the afternoon they enter the city, thirteen thousand strong. The Capital Police will cordon off a route and escort them the whole way. They'll come down Ninth Street to the Mall, swing right and march to the Washington Monument, then turn right again to fill the Ellipse. The White House gates will then be opened to allow them to fill the south lawn. Then you will appear on the balcony outside the Yellow Room and welcome them to Washington."

"The balcony? Listen, I've got to get closer to them than that. I've got to shake some little kid's hand. If I don't meet them face to face, I'll look like a fool."

"Of course. We'll get that girl who is the spokesperson up there with you. Frieda Caldwell, her name is. She'll give her cute little speech, and then it will be your turn."

"She's not the little kid with the flag, is she?" said the President nervously.

"Oh, no. This kid is a tough little cooky with a megaphone. She's no threat. We'll bring her in through the Diplomatic Reception Room. We've got a whole company of Marines in full parade dress blues to guard all the rest of the entrances, to keep that other kid out."

"All right." The President wiped his tired eyes. "So I'm to give a speech. What do you suggest I say?"

Charley laughed. "Oh, there's nothing to it.

You could give it blindfolded, right now, without any notes. You know the sort of thing. You'll congratulate this girl Frieda, and say what a fine young woman she is, the very pride of our nation, and how proud you are of our idealistic young people, and how much you share their cherished dreams for a world at peace, and how deeply impressed you have been by their courageous journey, and how grateful you are that in this land of liberty our young people care enough to bring their concerns to the nation's capital. And then you'll have a chance to present your own point of view, and say how tragic it is that in this dangerous world their idealism is still only a hope, a shining beacon for the future, because now, alas, we must depend on the strong defenders provided for us by modern science."

"Charley, you're a genius."

"And then we bring on the picnic and the fireworks." Charley got up and touched a button on the President's desk. "Mrs. Colefax, is the picnic all arranged?"

"Oh, yes, Mr. Chase." The tiny intercom crackled with the noise of rustling paper. Mrs. Colefax was reading from a list. "Twenty-five thousand hot dogs, three thousand cases of soft drinks, seven thousand pounds of ice, thirty thousand—"

"Good, good," said Charley. "Thank you, Mrs. Colefax." He turned back to the President. "And then we wow 'em with the fireworks display and at last they climb onto their buses and go home to Arkansas and Vermont and Illinois and Massachusetts and we never lay eyes on them again, and we can forget about the whole long tiresome nightmare."

"Buses? You've arranged for buses to spirit them out of town? Don't you think that's a little highhanded?"

"Oh, no, not me." Charley threw up his hands. "Their parents. They've organized the whole thing. I guess they're anxious to get their little darlings back." Then Charley sat down and reached forward to tap the President's knee. "But I've left the best till last. How about this? While the entire nation is watching the children on television and listening to little Frieda's speech and your own address to the Children's Crusade, that missile in Nevada can just *very quietly* leave the launching pad."

"You mean we could launch the missile at the same time?"

"During the fireworks. A little fireworks of our own, out there in Nevada. Why not? It's ready to go. The crew is only waiting for the signal to go

ahead. Naturally we won't announce it until all
the little kids have left town. All the protesters,
both young and old, will have shot their bolt.
They'll be worn out. And the missile will be up
there in outer space, doing its job. The thing will
be done."

"Well, congratulations," said the President
weakly, aware that he should be sounding more
enthusiastic. "All right. Why don't you hop over
to the Pentagon right now and explain it to General Sedgewick? Tell him I agree. Tell him to go
ahead."

"Very good, sir." Charley got up and made his
farewells and strode to the door.

As soon as he was gone the President took off
his shoes and collapsed on the sofa. His head was
pounding. His mind felt clawed at, torn, and
bleeding. Once again he tried to summon all the
arguments for launching the Peace Missile. But
the arguments wouldn't arrange themselves in an
orderly progression. Instead they whirled around
and rose in spirals and collided in his brain. They
were so complicated, and they had to be worded
so carefully or else they sounded ridiculous, even
to himself.

The President moaned, and rolled over on the
sofa. He thought once again about the Children's

Crusade, bearing down upon him on the highway south of Baltimore. The children were saying something too, but it wasn't complicated at all. It was perfectly simple. It was

one simple tremendous truth.

He closed his eyes. He was worn out. He hadn't been able to sleep lately, not with all those thousands of little kids tramping through his head. Thousands of little children. *Except ye turn, and become as little children . . .*

Except ye turn—except ye turn . . .

The Last Camp

Oliver Winslow had picked up something else in Hubie's Discount Electronix Store in Washington. He had bought a public address system, on sale, cheap. The speechmaking arrangements for the last camp were going to be different from all the rest. Frieda's voice was going to be heard by every single one of the thirteen thousand members of the Children's Crusade.

They were spending the night on the grounds of the Agricultural Research Center in Beltsville, Maryland. In the lobby of the Administration Building Oliver found a convenient electrical outlet, and he got to work hooking up his public address system.

The Agricultural Research Center was only ten miles from Washington.

Supper was a miracle. It was provided by vol-

unteers from the Nutrition Research Center at
Beltsville and the Home Economics Department
at the University of Maryland, and by a lot of
cooks from some of the army units at Fort Meade.
After supper, when the last of the paper plates
and plastic forks had been gathered up in trash
bags and carried away, Frieda mounted the steps
of the Administration Building and stood between the lofty columns and picked up Oliver's
microphone.

By now Frieda was an old hand at crowd command. She held the mike close to her face like a
rock star, and her voice reached to the last faraway cluster of pilgrims sitting cross-legged on
the grass.

"I THINK YOU WILL BE GLAD TO HEAR,"
said Frieda, her voice booming across Route 1
and the Baltimore and Ohio railroad tracks, all
the way to the cows grazing in a distant field,
"THAT OUR TOTAL IS NOW THIRTEEN
THOUSAND EIGHT HUNDRED NINETY-
SEVEN AND A HALF." There were whistles of
amazement. Thirteen thousand eight hundred
and ninety-six pairs of hands applauded. "THE
HALF IS OF COURSE OUR OFFICIAL PIL-
GRIMAGE BABY, CARRINGTON UPDIKE."
Frieda was really good at getting laughs. "NOW

I WANT TO REPEAT THE RULES FOR OUR MARCH INTO WASHINGTON TOMORROW. WE JUST MARCH QUIETLY BEHIND THE CAPITAL POLICE ESCORT, OKAY? IF ANYBODY YELLS SOMETHING MEAN AT US, WE DON'T YELL ANYTHING BACK. NO SHOVING WHEN WE ENTER THE WHITE HOUSE GATES. OH, AND WE'RE GONG TO SING. SIDNEY, YOU WANT US TO PRACTICE? HEY, SIDNEY? WHERE'S SIDNEY? OH, THERE HE IS! COME ON, SIDNEY! OKAY, EVERYBODY, HERE'S SIDNEY!"

Sidney Bloom took the microphone from Frieda, and then his voice too was echoing to the chickens in the poultry houses and the cows in the field. "HEY, EVERYBODY, LISTEN TO THIS. SOMEBODY TELLS ME WE'VE GOT A BAND, THE BELTSVILLE JUNIOR HIGH SCHOOL BAND. IS THAT RIGHT? WILL THE BAND PLEASE STAND UP?"

Everybody looked around, and then they all cheered. The Beltsville Junior High School Band was standing up in its green uniforms and beginning to play "The Stars and Stripes For Ever." Called upon without warning, they were off-key, but they were loud. The clarinets squawked, the cymbals clashed, the trumpets blared, the piccolo trilled, the bass drum thumped, and the great bashed bell of the sousaphone glittered and swayed. The massed thousands of crusaders applauded wildly, and whistled through their teeth.

"BEFORE I FORGET IT," said Frieda, taking over the mike again, flipping through her notes, "ELEANOR HALL WANTS TO KNOW IF PINKIE GARBER'S BIG SISTER MICHELLE IS HERE ANYWHERE. WILL MICHELLE PLEASE COME TO THE MICROPHONE? NOW, THE NEXT ITEM IS"—Frieda dropped her notes and picked them up—"BATHS."

There was an outbreak of derisive catcalls. "LISTEN," pleaded Frieda, "TOMORROW IS OUR BIG DAY. OF COURSE I KNOW THERE AREN'T ENOUGH SHOWERS HERE, BUT, PLEASE, EVERYBODY, GET AS CLEAN AS YOU CAN, OKAY?"

Eddy seized the microphone. "HEY, LISTEN, I THINK WE SHOULD BE DIRTY TOMORROW. I MEAN IT'S HONEST DIRT, RIGHT? WE PICKED IT UP IN ALL THOSE STATES WE WALKED THROUGH, DIDN'T WE? WHY DON'T WE HANG ON TO IT?"

There were loud screams of agreement and insane shrieks.

Frieda tactfully let the matter ride.

Below Eddy and Frieda at the microphone, Eleanor and Georgie and Cissie were huddled together on the steps of the Administration Building. Carrington lay drowsily in his buggy, holding Bingo. A small wistful child sat in Eleanor's lap, clinging to Eleanor's neck. It was Pinkie Garber, lost from her sister. Suddenly Pinkie gave a loud sob and sprang off Eleanor's knees and hurled herself at a cross-looking girl who was picking her way through the first row of crusaders at the foot of the steps.

"Where *were* you? said Michelle angrily. "I've been looking for you all *over* the place."

Robert was coming through the crowd, too, stepping carefully through a forest of signs from the Mount Pleasant Junior High School in Holly Oak, Delaware.

Eleanor looked at him expectantly. But Robert wanted to talk to Georgie. He sat down beside her and looked at her gravely. "Listen, Georgie," he said, "let's talk about tomorrow."

PART THREE

The only deterrent to global war is military strength. When this powerful new weapon is launched to orbit the earth, we will at last achieve real superiority in the arms race with the Soviet Union. . . .

James R. Toby
President of the United States
The White House
Washington, D.C.

Stop, stop, stop. . . .

Georgie Hall
Grade 4
Alcott School
Concord, Massachusetts

The End of Route 1

— ☆ —

In Baltimore and Harrisburg and Philadelphia and Alexandria and Richmond, people got up early and packed lunches and drove to Washington. They lined the avenues along the line of march, pushing forward on the sidewalks, competing for the best places to watch the arrival of the Children's Crusade.

The people who worked in Washington had the day off. They thronged the stairways of the government buildings.

Senators and members of congress and judges of the Supreme Court were crowded in with everybody else. There were no special arrangements for important people.

Along the line of march the streets were roped off. They were empty of traffic. Every now and then a forbidden Fourth of July firecracker landed

255

on the pavement, with a *spitter-spat* of exploding ladyfingers.

"Here they come!" The news ran down the street. By one o'clock the first ranks of the Children's Crusade were passing Mt. Vernon Square. The avenue was called Ninth Street in Washington, but the route markers still said ⑴ . It was the same highway that had brought them all the way from Massachusetts, from Rhode Island and Connecticut, through New York City and New Jersey and Pennsylvania and Maryland. Now it was setting them down gently at their destination.

But instead of shopping malls and gasoline stations and fast-food drive-ins, there were majestic buildings of white marble on this part of Route 1, with columned porches and magnificent stairways. The fourteen thousand members of the Children's Crusade flooded the avenue for two miles, pouring thickly toward the south, marching twelve abreast, their faces beaming, their flags waving, their signs bobbing up and down to show who they were and where they came from—*Mark Twain Elementary School in Hannibal, Missouri; Mary McLeod Bethune Junior High School in Daytona Beach, Florida; Riverside Middle School in Bismarck, North Dakota;* and, of course, *Mrs. Hussey's Sixth Grade*

Class, George W. Palmer Elementary School, Jethro, Illinois, was present one hundred percent.

First in line was the Beltsville Junior High School Band. The drummer walloped his drum and the sousaphone player filled his cheeks with air and puckered his lips and blew until the buildings echoed with his mighty *PAH, PAH, PAH, OOM-PAH.* Right behind the band came Sidney, walking backward, hurling his arms over his head to encourage the marching thousands to sing. Obediently they tried, joyously and loud, and the song worked its way back for block after block in shrill waves of musical noise.

They were all very dirty. The dirt was thickest at shoe level. Their socks were stiff with it. Their shorts and jeans were greasy. Their shirts were streaked with gray. Their faces were more or less clean, but dirt was ground into the folds of their eyelids and the curled passages of their ears. Their hair was filthy—except for Eleanor's, which had been washed in the ladies' room of an Amoco station in Hyattsville.

But the dirt was a proud badge. It was honest dirt, as Eddy had said, won by hard pounding on the road.

Some of the pilgrims were much cleaner than the rest. They were new recruits, two thousand of them, lunging into the street from the sidewalk, thrilled to be walking the last few blocks with the Children's Crusade, while their mothers screamed after them, "Where will I find you?" The old hands swung along beside the new ones in the full swashbuckling pride of their grubbiness, and snickered a little at the bright clean shirts and the blazing white sneakers. Harper Flint was a new recruit, and he felt their scorn. Swiftly he tore off the seersucker jacket his mother had bought him in Portland, and wrenched off his necktie, and rolled up his oxford-cloth shirtsleeves.

No one could accuse Carrington Updike of being a Johnny-come-lately. Carrington rolled along at the front of the line, the wheels of his dusty stroller squealing while he laughed and chuckled and bestowed jolly greetings left and right. Behind him, Cissie walked in glory, the proud sister of the dirtiest and most famous baby in the entire United States.

The Two Flags Meet
at Last

— ☆ —

The President could feel them coming. The walls
of the White House were closing in around him.
It was a besieged fortress. At every door a Marine
stood at attention in full ceremonial parade dress
blues. The television networks had been forbidden entry. The TV people were fooling around
outside, running their cables across the lawn.

From the windows of the Yellow Room on the
second floor the President could see the children
of the crusade. They were flowing toward him
across the Ellipse. As far away as the Washington
Monument he could see nothing but children.

It was a horrifying sight. Once again the President wished with all his heart that they were a
battalion of enemy soldiers or a horde of angry
adults. But they were not. They were infants, not
infantry, and that was the whole trouble. They

were children, not grown-ups. And it was *because* they were young that they were strong. Their might lay in their round cheeks, their soft budlike noses, their lack of stature, their small wiry arms and legs, their—the President groaned and turned away from the window—their *innocence.* How on earth could he fight back against innocence?

Charley Chase came running in, carrying the Presidential flag. "I'm sorry, sir, but I can't find that kid, Harper Flint. I found the flag outside the Oval Office, leaning against the door. Where can that boy be?"

"You can't find him? That's terrible. I need him. I can't go out on that balcony alone." And then the President's face lit up with surprise and relief. "Oh, Robert, there you are! Thank heaven! It's about time."

His grandson stood in the doorway. He was not alone. A small thin girl was standing beside him, carrying a flag.

Robert looked at his grandfather soberly. "This is the new flag bearer," he said, giving Georgie a gentle shove.

The President was puzzled. "But I thought that boy from Maine still had a couple of days to go."

"No," said Robert, shaking his head firmly. "Harper's gone. It's her turn now. She's from Massachusetts."

"Oh," said the President. "Well, all right. That explains why we couldn't find Harper." He reached down to shake Georgie's hand and smile at her. "Welcome to the White House, my dear."

"Here, honey," said Charley Chase, holding out the Presidential flag. "You've got the wrong flag. This is the one you should be carrying."

The little girl looked anxious. She clung tightly to the staff of her own flag.

"No, no," said Robert quickly. "Her flag's okay."

"But this is the one the kids are supposed to—" Charley paused in midsentence, staring at the little girl's flag. His own drooped in his hand. The two flags leaned toward each other, and then the gold eagle on the top of the Presidential flag touched the top of Georgie's. At once a shiver ran through the stiff folds of the sparkling banner in Charley's hand. The staff snapped. The flag fell to the floor. Embarrassed, he picked it up and looked at it in surprise. The sparkles were falling in a gold shower on the rug. The flag was disintegrating in his hand.

Georgie spoke up bravely. "Would you like to hear my letter?" she said, looking soberly at the President.

"Your letter?" Restlessly the President glanced out the window. The front rank of children was drawn up across the driveway, waiting for the thousands of their companions to squeeze through the White House gates and spread out over the south lawn. A small person was walking up and down with a megaphone. Through the open window the President could hear her. She was shouting orders.

"Why, yes, of course I'd like to hear your letter," he said, turning back to Georgie. Then he winked at Charley Chase and sat down on an antique chair. He was grateful for the presence of the new flag bearer. Now he would be able to walk out on the balcony in the company of his grandson and the child from Massachusetts. He wouldn't be just one mean, ornery grown-up standing there alone, in opposition to all the cute little kids in the world.

Georgie cleared her throat and reached into her shirt pocket for her letter. It was rumpled, and nearly worn through at the fold lines. She stood in front of the center window, holding the letter in one hand and the staff of her flag in the other, and began to read. Her voice was nervous and hurried, but light and clear.

Her letter was exactly what Eleanor had thought, an ordinary fourth-grade letter, inscribed in pencil on a sheet of lined notebook paper. But Georgie had written it with passion.

Listening to it, the President was mildly surprised. It was different from the letters of the other winners. This child had not written about the wonders of her own home state, like Susan Hobbs and Dubose Boudreau and David Klein and Maria Verdade and Harper Flint. To the little girl from Massachusetts the flag of the United States meant a world without nuclear weapons. Her letter was a plea on behalf of the green earth.

It was just the sort of letter that had been ruled out by Mrs. Linda Goodspeed. The President was astonished that Mrs. Goodspeed should have chosen it. But he sat politely in his chair, listening, idly watching the folds of the child's flag lift and curl in the light draft from the window.

It was a beautiful flag, thought the President, even though there were no gold messages written across it, and no screaming eagle at the top of the staff. The stars on the field of blue were tumbling over one another as though the heavens themselves were waltzing, and the broad stripes billowed like dancing hills and valleys.

Then the breeze from the window strengthened, and the flag blew out to its full length and hung there, trembling, suspended in the gushing air from out-of-doors.

The flag filled the President's vision. It was all

he could see, the blue field with its white stars and the quivering stripes of red and white. He felt a little faint. Before his eyes the swaying fabric was turning into ocean waves, rippling and flowing, purling in dimpled swirls and bubbles. It was a swelling current in the sea, carrying a tide of vessels to the shore. And childen were pouring off the great ships and tipping out of small boats onto the sloping beach. Then before his eyes the water shimmered out of sight behind tall buildings, and the President could see light streaking between towering structures, blinding rays streaming down narrow streets where children were moving in a flood, their shoulders massed together, rocking left and right. They were thick in a hundred thousand school yards. They were everywhere.

The President drew a deep breath, as he understood. He understood at last. The country he governed was not a land of soldiers and sailors and fighter pilots. It was not a nation of Democrats and Republicans. It was a mighty swarm of children, eager to suck into their lungs the clear bright air, to yell and catcall and laugh and shout, to spring off the ground and come down hard, to grow to their full height. It was kids, millions of kids, budding and ripening, sprouting and blossoming, kids in their heyday, their springtime, their green prime, hungry for the good things of this earth that were their due. It was a new flock of children every day, tossed up and flung kicking, as high and far as old arms could hurl them. They were spinning seeds exploding from the tree of the present moment, sent whirling into the future as far as the winds would blow. They were careless and hopeful and greedy, they were grinning and expectant, healthy and strong, and altogether worthwhile.

And then the President staggered to his feet. Before his eyes the flag was splitting asunder. There was a terrible roar and a flash of blinding light. He tottered, and grasped at the draperies of the window. The noise was deafening, a continuous explosion, a thunderous, massive booming cannonade like the fall of cities, the collapse of mountain ranges, the eruption of volcanoes. Horror-struck, he stared out the window at the south lawn. The children were gone. Something menacing and terrible was happening. A crimson wave was rolling toward the south portico, throwing itself forward, rushing at the building in which he stood. It was a blood-red wave, a great comber of blood with a curling crest, dashing itself at the pillars of the colonnade. Frantically he slammed down the sash, just as the wave splashed against it and ran down the glass in scarlet drops.

Gasping, the President stumbled away. The wave collapsed. Swiftly it was sucked backward and out of sight. The thundering noise diminished, the fiery pall of smoke was gone. Once more the sun was shining, the grass was green, the window was clean and transparent. But blood was still cupped in the curved scrolls of the Ionic capitals. The President could still see it there, trapped in little wells in the petals of the carved roses.

Charley Chase took the President's arm. "Are you all right, sir?" he said. "You look ill."

The President stared at Charley. Charley's face, too, was gray. Then President Toby pulled himself together and straightened up. "No, no, I'm not ill. I'm all right." He turned once again to the little girl from Massachusetts.

She had finished reading her letter. Her flag hung slack, its shuddering folds nearly touching the floor. Robert leaned against a window frame. He was gazing at nothing, just as usual.

The President squared his shoulders and turned once again to the window. Outdoors the trees were spreading their round globes of leaves, the sun was shining on the flowering shrubs and borders, and thousands of children were streaming across the driveway. Their faces were turned up to the window anxiously, as if they were asking a question, a single question, one terribly important question to which they had to have an answer, and they had to have it now.

"Come on," said the President to Georgie and Robert. "I've got to talk to them."

Charley Chase followed him out onto the balcony. Charley was in a state of confusion. All his fixed notions of what the President was going to say to the Children's Crusade had gone out of his head. What was it that he had suggested? He couldn't remember.

The President's prepared speech was neatly folded in the inside pocket of his suit jacket. He left it there. He looked down at Eleanor and Eddy and Frieda and Cissie and Carringon and Sidney and Weezie and Oliver and all the rest of the sixteen thousand children of the Crusade, spread out before him in a great host, all the way to the Mall and the Washington Monument, and beyond the Monument to the Tidal Basin of the Potomac River.

He put his hand on the microphone and spoke into it, trying to reach as many as he could with his strong voice. "All right," he said. "I agree. You're right. I'll do what I can."

Charley Chase was astonished to discover that his eyes were wet. When the President turned to him and nodded gravely, Charley knew at once what he meant. He slipped indoors and sought out a particular telephone and put through a call to Nevada. "Cancel it," he said. "Just call the whole thing off."

Below the balcony on the White House lawn, Eleanor was crushed between Frieda and Cissie. She couldn't believe what she had heard. She looked at Frieda, who was dumbfounded too.

"What did he say?" said Derek Cherniak. The network cameras had been set up in the wrong place, directly beneath the President on the balcony of the first floor. The cameramen and the audio people were dazed. They heard the joyous shriek run backward through the horde of children massed in front of them. What was going on?

But of course it was the good news passing from the front rank to the rear, like a ripple in a pond, like the wildfire spread of gossip.

"Did he really say it?" shouted Cissie to Eleanor. "Do you think he really means it?"

"Look at Robert," cried Eleanor happily. "Look at Georgie."

Robert was looking down at them, grinning

and waving. Georgie's face was shining. Her flag was fluttering in a glad romp of red, white, and blue.

Derek Cherniak ran down the curving stairs from the first-floor balcony to the lawn and got the news at second hand. Then he poked his microphone at Frieda.

"How does it feel to be a hero?" he said, and then he corrected himself gracefully. "Excuse me, I mean heroine."

Frieda gave him a pitying look. "I'm a hero-person," she said crisply, and tramped away to find Sidney.

Back into the Grove
of Trees

— ☆ —

In the confusion that followed it was a miracle no one was hurt. The President came downstairs with Georgie and Robert and walked out onto the lawn and shook hundreds of dirty hands. He talked to flabbergasted newsmen. He picked up Carrington and tossed him playfully in the air. He clapped Harper Flint on the back. He spoke kindly to Eleanor and signed the autograph book Frieda whipped out of her knapsack.

Eleanor's head was spinning. She nearly lost her balance when she was kissed by Robert Toby and clasped around the knees by Weezie Hoskins at the same time.

"I don't want to go home," sobbed Weezie, hanging on like grim death.

Flushed and excited, Eleanor smiled at Robert and took Weezie by the shoulders. Would her duties never end? "Listen, Weezie, it won't be so bad. Georgie and Frieda, they'll be your friends. And you can come over to our house lots of times, okay?"

Weezie sniffled and cheered up, and then it was Eleanor's turn to burst into tears, as two familiar people held out their arms to her.

"Aunt Alex, Uncle Fred." Eleanor felt the ground lurch under her feet. A moment ago she had been substitute mother to hundreds and hundreds of fidgety little kids. Now she was once more a person with a mother of her own—well, an aunt who was as good as a mother. For the first time in six weeks she didn't have to wonder if some careless urchin would get sick or dart into the road. She didn't have to be a super-baby-sitter with thousands of charges. She could be a baby herself if she wanted. Eleanor leaned against Uncle Freddy and sobbed.

"Eleanor, *dear*," said Aunt Alex, "whatever is the matter?"

"I'm so glad," wept Eleanor. "I'm just so glad."

They went back to Concord, and life returned to normal. Georgie stepped back into her grove of trees. Eddy helped Oliver Winslow install a rebuilt engine in the Green Horror. Together the two of them lowered it into the Chevy with a chain thrown over the branch of a tree. Eleanor had her ears pierced and went bowling with Robert Toby. She felt older, years older than she had been last May when the march began. But that was nothing new. Eleanor was always looking back with astonishment at the great gulfs that had opened up between the person she was now and the one she had been only a short time before.

The old flag was back in the attic. After all its travels, it seemed none the worse for wear. But it was still very fragile, so Georgie and Uncle Freddy folded it up, star against star, stripe against stripe, and put it safely back in the cardboard box.

"We can always get it out if we want it," Uncle Freddy said. "Someday we might need it again. I hope not, but you never can tell."

As for the President, he kept his promise. He stopped the launching of the Peace Missile. And after that he did his best to help the cause. It's true that his resolve sometimes faltered. But whenever that happened, he had a remedy. He simply walked up the grand staircase to the Yellow Room on the second floor, and looked out the window at the capitals of the great pillars of the south portico.

And there he could always see what he expected to see. Blood was still cupped in the scrolls of the Ionic capitals. It never disappeared. It was always there, and would be, he suspected, forever.

> My story is a fable.
> No one is encouraged
> to set off along the
> highway, even to save
> the world.

ABOUT THE AUTHOR

JANE LANGTON is the author of eight books for young people, including four other fantasies about the Hall family of Concord: THE DIAMOND IN THE WINDOW, THE SWING IN THE SUMMERHOUSE, THE ASTONISHING STEREOSCOPE, and the 1981 Newbery Honor Book THE FLEDGLING. Ms. Langton is also well known in the world of children's literature for her many articles and reviews in *The Horn Book* and *The New York Times Book Review*.

Born in Boston, Massachusetts, Ms. Langton studied astronomy at Wellesley College and the University of Michigan and did graduate work in the history of art at the University of Michigan and Radcliffe College. She now lives in Lincoln, Massachusetts, with her husband, Bill. They have three grown-up sons.